Adam moved menacingly nearer

"So you want to play in the snow, do you?" He scooped up snow from the railing and washed B.J.'s face.

She turned and quickly packed another snowball, then pitched it with deadly accuracy. It caught him on the side of the head.

Adam caught her by the arm before she could throw a second one. She nearly pulled free, but the hand gripping her arm was too strong. With no effort, he hauled her against him. She could feel the warmth of his body.

"You thought you had the advantage because my arm's in a cast," he said in a low tone.

"I'll take any advantage I can." B.J.'s breath was coming in short gasps.

"Then be warned. So will I."

Dear Reader:

Nora Roberts, Tracy Sinclair, Jeanne Stephens, Carole Halston, Linda Howard. Are these authors familiar to you? We hope so, because they are just a few of our most popular authors who publish with Silhouette Special Edition each and every month. And the Special Edition list is changing to include new writers with fresh stories. It has been said that discovering a new author is like making a new friend. So during these next few months, be sure to look for books by Sandi Shane, Dorothy Glenn and other authors who have just written their first and second Special Editions, stories we hope you enjoy.

Choosing which Special Editions to publish each month is a pleasurable task, but not an easy one. We look for stories that are sophisticated, sensuous, touching, and great love stories, as well. These are the elements that make Silhouette Special Editions more romantic...and unique.

So we hope you'll find this Silhouette Special Edition just that—*Special*—and that the story finds a special place in your heart.

The Editors at Silhouette

SERL-7/85

RUTH LANGAN
Star-Crossed

Silhouette Special Edition

Published by Silhouette Books New York

America's Publisher of Contemporary Romance

To my daughter Carol,
the actress.

SILHOUETTE BOOKS
300 E. 42nd St., New York, N.Y. 10017

Copyright © 1985 by Ruth Langan

Distributed by Pocket Books

ISBN: 0-373-09266-0

First Silhouette Books printing October 1985

10 9 8 7 6 5 4 3 2 1

America's Publisher of Contemporary Romance

Printed in the U.S.A.

RUTH LANGAN

loves to create independent heroines and heroes who can be both tough and tender. A sense of humor is a necessary quality in her characters.

Married to her childhood sweetheart, she has five children, two dogs, two cats and thrives on both her careers.

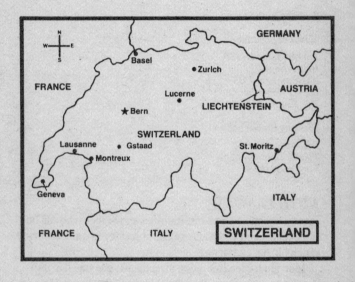

Chapter One

You really intend to go through with this, don't you?" The man's voice was a low growl, made even deeper by anxiety.

The elderly woman stared at her son for several seconds without responding. For one brief moment, in her mind's eye, he was her little boy again, staring wide-eyed at the photographers while she shielded him from the glare of their flashbulbs. Now he was a man, living a vastly different life from hers. For years their only communication was hurried letters, or static-blurred phone calls from distant countries with exotic names. And he was now the one trying to shield her.

It tore at her heart to see him so concerned about her. It was bad enough that a wide swath of dressing covered the stitches in his forehead, which was now further marred by a frown. It distressed her to note the left arm enclosed in a cast, resting close to his chest in a sling. The right hand was clenched at his side. That was the nature of family, she thought with a sigh. They were so closely bound. It was inevitable that they worried about each other, hurt for each other.

Her clear blue gaze met his stern gray look. She nodded in response to his question and sat down stiffly at her desk. His eyes narrowed as he watched her movement, and she was reminded again how like his father he was. So dedicated to his work. Able to shut out everything that might interfere with his concentration. And yet unbelievably kind, so determined to protect her from the cruelty that was inevitable.

"And you, Flynn?" he said to the tall woman who hovered at her side. "Can't you make her see what a terrible mistake this is?"

"I've tried, Adam. You know there's no reasoning with your mother when her mind's made up. I—" Her head came up sharply at the sound of the telephone. She lifted the receiver before the second ring.

"Yes?" She paused, listening, then cut off the speaker with a brusque "Yes. Send her up."

Her voice was a monotone. "That—reporter is here."

For one awful moment, there was no sound in the room. With a quick glance of concern at the older woman, her secretary clamped her mouth firmly shut on anything further she might have said, and strode from the room. As her footsteps echoed along the hall, mother and son turned and eyed each other before once more breaking the silence.

B.J. Conover turned up the collar of her camel's hair coat against the bitter gust of wind from the East River. It had been a fairly mild November, but now, midway through the month, the weather had turned sullen. The sky was leaden, and there was the bite of snow in the air. B.J. shivered and studied the plush New York apartment building that loomed before her. Her agent had intruded on her much-needed vacation in the Florida sun to summon her home for the assignment of a lifetime. Nora London, the reclusive movie actress who had not granted an interview in thirty-seven years, had asked to meet with her. Her. And all because her latest book, *So Dear*, about the life of silent screen star Vernon Allmon, had apparently piqued the curiosity or, she thought with a smile, the discriminating taste of the great lady.

B.J. tucked an errant strand of auburn hair behind her ear. She had spent the five hours on the plane devouring everything she could about Nora London. The newspaper headlines alone were enough to fill a book. From her first movie in 1932, which thrust her into instant stardom, the actress had captured the imagination of the public and the press. She was the only star known equally by either name. "Nora lights up the screen in *Heartsong*." London snags top role in *The Pirate* with Stephen Hart.

Then in 1947, when Hollywood's leading lady completed her thirteenth movie, she dropped out of sight to give birth to her only child. She refused to reveal the name of her lover, but it was widely reported that she had had a sizzling romance with her leading man during the filming of her last picture. He had made endless movies of romantic fantasy and adventure, and his off-screen life was rumored to be like that of a dashing swashbuckler as well.

The press had a field day. Although Stephen Hart never admitted paternity, he never denied it either. His oft quoted response was, "I'm rumored to have children all over the globe, but of course, that's part and parcel of being a star." With a careless shrug, he was photographed waving and flashing his most charming smile to the camera.

Photographers hounded the reclusive woman, even camping out on her doorstep in a rural cottage in France, to capture a picture of anyone who visited her. They were disappointed to see only a doctor and a nurse and one or two of her most devoted friends. All but her most loyal fans deserted her. She was branded a scarlet woman. Her career in movies was finished. To this day, Nora London had never revealed the name of her son's father. She had never married. She had never returned to Hollywood, dividing her time instead between her apartment in New York, a home outside Paris, and a chalet in Gstaad. And she had steadfastly avoided giving an interview—until today.

Inside the plush building B.J. gave her name to a security man and waited while he phoned for clearance. On the elevator she turned down the collar of her coat and nervously ran her hands through the thick russet hair that fell in soft tangles to her shoulders. When the elevator came to a smooth stop, she took a deep breath to steady her nerves. What do you say when you're introduced to a legend?

When the apartment door opened, she faced a tall woman with coal-black hair pulled back in a severe bun. Rimless glasses intensified unblinking dark eyes. She appeared to be in her mid-fifties. A designer suit of navy wool looked fashionable on her reed-slim figure.

"Miss Conover?" The voice was clipped, professional.

"Yes."

The woman extended her hand. "Nancy Flynn. Miss London's secretary. She'll see you in the library."

The handshake was brisk, businesslike. But the eyes, B.J. noted, were cold and unsmiling. Chalk up one person who wasn't happy about this interview.

As she followed the woman, B.J. heard the muted rumble of voices, low, tinged with emotion. Stepping into a book-lined room, she was greeted by a sudden, awkward silence.

A fire crackled invitingly. There was, all about her, the wonderful scent of old leather and books. Walls of books. B.J. was aware of all these things, but her gaze riveted on the woman behind the desk. The hair, once as dark as a raven's, was now white and softened by a hairdresser's tints. But the face was unmistakable. That face! That ageless, amazing, fabulous face, which had stared out from countless yellowed newspapers and magazines. She had once had the exotic features of a temptress. At seventy-two, she was soft, plump, pink—and still beautiful.

Two years earlier, on the thirty-fifth anniversary of her last film, a university in New York had held a month-long retrospective, showing all her films and honoring her with an award. The reclusive actress had sent her regrets that she would be unable to attend.

The woman stood, and B.J. was surprised to note that she was no taller than her own five feet four inches. Somehow, she had expected a giant. Her dress was pale peach, in a soft wool, with a matching cardigan jacket of darker peach cashmere. The shade enhanced her white hair and added color to her soft skin.

Extending a smooth, well-manicured hand, the famous actress smiled. "Miss Conover. How nice of you to come."

B.J. swallowed down the laugh that bubbled in her throat. How nice? Wild horses couldn't have kept her away. *How nice of you to invite me,* she thought of responding. But that would be totally inane. *How wildly wonderful to have this rare opportunity* would be more appropriate. B.J. was dying of curiosity. She had a million questions she wanted to hurl at this mysterious woman. But this was Nora London's show. She'd let her play it her way.

"Miss London. It's a pleasure to meet you." B.J. wondered if her voice betrayed her nerves.

The handshake was cordial, sincere. The older woman turned slightly toward the man who stood to her right, half in shadow. "Miss Conover, this is my son, Adam."

He stepped forward to offer his hand. B.J. felt her breath catch in her throat as the light from the fire played over him. In that brief instant she glimpsed a lean, well-muscled figure in worn denims and a plaid shirt with one sleeve cut out to accommodate a plaster cast. Several days' growth of beard darkened his face, adding to his craggy appearance. A white gauze bandage covered his forehead and was a startling contrast to dark, shaggy hair badly in need of a trim. Penetrating gray eyes coolly appraised her.

From the little she knew of him, he was nearly as fascinating a character as his famous mother. A widely respected photojournalist and foreign correspondent, for years he had been reporting bloody wars around the globe. His name, if not his face, was familiar to millions of Americans, as he covered the battles that raged in the Middle East, Central America, Africa and Northern Ireland.

"Hello, Adam." She was aware of his hand engulfing hers, warm and firm, while his sharp gaze continued to hold hers. She was shocked at the strong sexual pull, as compelling as an electrical jolt. In the depths of his steel gaze, she felt he was aware of it, too.

When he broke contact, she felt shaken. She had expected a star of the stature of Nora London to dominate the room. But this son of hers was definitely her equal.

"Please, Miss Conover. Sit here." Nora indicated a pair of leather, high-backed chairs that faced the enormous desk. While her son held her chair, she seated herself.

She smiled and peered at the young woman. B.J. openly studied her as well, deciding immediately that she saw honesty and great strength in that remarkably unlined face. But around the eyes she could detect vulnerability. This woman might have been a survivor, but she had been deeply hurt as well.

"What does the B.J. stand for?"

"Bernadette Jessica. Bernadette Jessica Conover," she said with thinly veiled distaste.

"Why don't you like it? It's a lovely name. You should always use it."

B.J. shrugged. "I suppose I decided it sounded too pretentious."

"I hope you won't mind if I call you Jessica. I can't imagine calling anyone as lovely as you B.J."

For the first time, B.J. laughed. She had a deep, husky voice, and her laughter had a rich, joyous tone. "You sound like my mother. She always called me Jessica. But I've been B.J. since I wrote my first book. My editor thought it would sell better if the readers thought I was a man."

"What was it about?"

With a chuckle, B.J. said, "It was a dry, literary piece about Bacon and Shakespeare. It probably sold a dozen copies. My relatives and friends were very supportive."

The actress shared her laughter. "But your picture was on the back page of your newest book. How can you hope to fool anyone?"

"By now my secret's out. After my second book my cover was blown. Now everyone knows B.J. Conover is a woman. But it's too late to change my pen name."

Disdaining a chair, Adam leaned a hip against the bookcase and studied this disarming young woman. He, too, had seen her picture on the book, but it hadn't prepared him for her vitality. The brief biography that accompanied the photo had merely given her age—twenty-eight—and her background. A degree in journalism from Michigan State University. Two years as editor with a major publishing house in New York before publication of her first book. There had been three more books since then, and each of them had received critical acclaim.

The photo didn't do her justice. He itched for a camera. In the dappled sunlight her hair was lush, dark, with fiery strands that caught and held the light. It was the kind of hair that men dreamed of, on long, moonlit nights in faraway lands. Her skin, too, looked kissed by the sun. She had obviously not been spending her time here in New York. The Sun Belt, he decided. Spending her days lazing around in a hammock. He could picture her swaying lazily, her nose stuck in a book. The eyes were green, crinkling when she laughed.

There was intelligence in them, and humor. She slipped out of her coat to reveal charcoal wool slacks and an ivory mohair sweater that hugged high, firm breasts and a narrow waist. Adam felt a rush of heat as he found himself wondering how she looked in a bikini. Surprised and a little angry at the direction of his thoughts, he clenched his fist and continued to stare openly.

B.J. was aware of Adam's scrutiny. She had sensed his curiosity, and even more, his hostility when she entered, and now, feeling his gaze burn over her, she had to force herself to concentrate on the reason for this visit. Her cheeks grew hot. She blamed it on the fire.

In the exchange that followed, she completely forgot Adam London and the secretary who discretly hovered near the door.

"I'm having some tea," the actress said. "Would you like some?"

"Yes, thank you."

Nora London picked up the phone and said, "Gerta, we'll have our tea now." Replacing the receiver, she continued, "I loved your book, *So Dear*, so much, I've read it twice."

B.J. blinked in surprise, then allowed a warm smile to spread across her features. "Thank you. That's the finest compliment you can give a writer. Did you know Vernon Allmon?"

The actress nodded. "I met him when I first went to Hollywood. He was very kind to me. But then, he was kind to everyone. He was probably one of the truly nicest men I ever knew." She leaned forward. "You know, so many of the stars in Hollywood jealously guarded their fame. They realized how fleeting it can be." Her voice lowered perceptibly. "There's always someone in the wings waiting for you to falter so they can take your place." She smiled. "But Vernon went out of his way to show me the ropes."

She smiled as a maid entered with a tray bearing a china tea service. "Thank you, Gerta. I'll pour."

The maid's plain features softened into a smile as she handed her employer a delicately embroidered linen napkin. Turning toward B.J., the woman's smile faded. She eyed her suspiciously before leaving the room.

B.J. suppressed a laugh. First the secretary, now the maid. The troops were circling the wagons, closing ranks around their leader, before the threatened attack. A reporter, even though an invited guest, was definitely the villain in this piece.

Nora continued as smoothly as if she hadn't been interrupted. "After a while, I'm sorry to say, Vernon and I lost contact. He signed on with a different studio. And when he shot that young starlet and took his own life, I was shocked and, I suppose, disappointed in him, but like everyone else, I just believed what I read in the papers at the time, and then eventually forgot about him."

She handed B.J. a cup of tea and a napkin. "Sugar or lemon?"

"Neither, thank you."

The actress looked across the room at her silent secretary. "Tea, Flynn?"

She shook her head.

"Adam? Tea?"

"No."

When B.J. glanced in his direction, she felt the cold stab of his direct look.

The actress sipped her drink a moment in silence, then said, "Your book brought out so many little things I had once known about Vernon. The private little charitable acts that no one ever read about. The honorable way he conducted himself when the studio sold his contract without even telling him. And that young girl, whom the papers had painted as the soul of innocence..." She paused, and for a moment her eyes met B.J.'s, and there was a hint of pain. "The fact is, your book forced me to think about things I hadn't wanted to think about. I began to question rumors I had begun to accept as fact. And more important, you made me care again about Vernon. You helped me understand what had happened to drive an honorable, gentle man like him to murder and suicide."

"That's why I chose to write the book, Miss London. To let the reader see the real Vernon Allmon."

"But why? What was he to you?" The blue eyes widened, as if pleading for an explanation.

"I happened to read something about him that caught my attention. I delved further and came up with a fascinating character. Before long, he had completely captured my imagination. I knew I had to write about this man. In his time he was one of the biggest stars in Hollywood."

The older woman nodded, her eyes taking on a faraway look. For long moments she stared at the desk top, deep in thought. Then she pulled herself back to the present.

"Do you have any idea why I wanted to meet you, Jessica?"

This was it. This was the end of the small talk. Now they would get down to business.

B.J. set her cup down and shook her head. "My agent said you wanted to meet with me. But he didn't know whether you would permit a transcript of the interview."

The actress smiled at her confusion. "No, Jessica. No transcript."

B.J.'s heart sank. A once in a lifetime chance, and she couldn't even keep a record of it.

"I want you to write an authorized biography of my life."

B.J.'s head came up sharply. For a moment she could only stare. "A book? You want me to write a book about your life?"

"Isn't that what you do best?" Nora's smile grew.

"But why?" Immediately B.J. lifted her hand as if to cancel the foolish question. "I mean, why me, and why now?"

"Because you have that rare talent, the ability to make the reader care about your subject. And because I want some control over what will be written about me—before it's too late." There was a muted sadness in her tone, before her acting talent surfaced and she managed a bright smile.

B.J. wondered how much honesty this woman would be able to endure. Taking a deep breath, she decided to take that first faltering step in their relationship. "I'm a meticulous researcher and a writer of nonfiction, Miss London. Once I've researched the facts, I won't be persuaded to change them around to suit your fancy. Even if those facts are painful." She gave the actress a meaningful stare and emphasized each word. "I don't write fiction."

B.J. felt the man stiffen, but she forced herself to continue to stare at his mother. The older woman's eyes never wavered as she continued to meet her look.

"I admire your integrity. I won't ask you to alter the facts, Jessica. But I want to be assured that you have the facts, and not some distorted version of them." She spread her hands. "I have diaries, journals, press clippings, scrapbooks. I think I have everything you need to write my biography."

"You'd want me to work here? But I have my own apartment."

Nora nodded. "Oh, but you should stay here. There's plenty of room. And it would save you the time of shuttling back and forth. The place is very big, even with the—unexpected presence of Adam." She turned wide eyes to him for a moment, and B.J. caught a momentary glimpse of the real affection between these two. "I'm sure you read of his accident in Central America?"

B.J. shook her head. "I'm afraid not. I've been on vacation. After spending so much time researching and writing, I've deliberately avoided television, newspapers or even a radio for the past week."

"His Jeep overturned. Adam says it was a minor accident. From what I've read, however, I understand he's lucky to be alive." Nora's voice was gently mocking. "He thinks he's fooled me into not worrying. But he knows better." Her smile grew. "He'll be here recuperating for a while."

"Not very long," his deep voice interrupted.

B.J. glanced at him. Though his face showed little emotion, there was a surprising warmth in his tone.

Nora said briskly, "You're staying as long as the doctor orders. And that's final." She turned her attention back to her guest. "You must stay here as well, Jessica. We have a lovely suite of rooms you can use. This way, we'll really get to know each other, and you'll have first-hand experience of how I live. You can have access to all my papers, and we can spend at least part of each day talking, if you'd like."

Holding up a sheaf of papers, she added, "My lawyer has drawn up all the necessary releases and contracts. Would you like to look them over?"

"No. They'd be Greek to me. I'll take them to my agent. He'll go over the fine points with me."

"Fine. Are you interested, Jessica?"

"I wouldn't be here if I weren't interested, Miss London." B.J.'s mind was whirling. This book could be a blockbuster. It could be her own ticket to fame. "I'll have my agent contact you."

"I'd like to get started as soon as possible. I only plan to be in New York for the season. Then I'd like to get back to Gstaad."

B.J. nodded. "Right. I'll call him this afternoon."

Standing, she picked up her coat and prepared to follow Flynn from the room. Extending her hand, she said, "Goodbye, Miss London. It's a very tantalizing offer. I hope it can be worked out to suit both of us."

"I hope so, too, Jessica."

B.J. nodded to Adam, hoping to avoid touching him again. "Goodbye."

"I'll see you to the door," he said, moving with surprising speed. Before either of the other two women could react, he propelled B.J. toward the front hall.

He closed the door and punched the elevator button. They stood stiffly, side by side, without a word. B.J. drew a deep breath, eager to escape this man who had glowered at her during the entire interview. When the elevator arrived, she felt a momentary surge of relief. Adam surprised her by stepping inside with her. In that little cocoon of privacy, safely out of hearing, she had the first taste of his controlled fury.

"I'm sure you can understand why this book about my mother is out of the question, Miss Conover."

Her mouth dropped open at his obvious hostility. "No. I can't understand. She appears to be an intelligent woman who knows exactly what she's doing."

"The publicity, after all these years, would kill her."

"It seems to me that she's given this considerable thought. Apparently this is what she wants."

He swore through gritted teeth. "I'm telling you, I want you to refuse to work with her on this project."

She bristled with anger. "You've picked the wrong person to try to intimidate, Adam. If your mother is determined to go ahead with this book,

I have no intention of talking her out of it. I suggest you take this up with her.''

"I intend to.'' Gingerly, he touched the arm encased in the plaster cast. "I've begun to think my accident was a very lucky break after all. If I weren't here to protect her from the vultures, she'd be in over her head before she realized what was happening.''

"Vultures...!''

The elevator came to a sudden stop at the lobby. Again Adam surprised her by stepping out beside her. Roughly taking her coat from her arm, he held it in his good hand. Apparently, she thought, even his anger couldn't erase the manners instilled from childhood. Slipping her arms into the sleeves, she felt the warmth of his touch where his fingers lingered at her neck. With a nervous gesture she shook her hair free, and it tumbled over her collar, brushing his hand.

Adam stopped short when he felt her hair sweep his skin. It was every bit as soft as it had looked in the firelight of the library. He fought the strange compelling urge to grab a handful of it. Stepping back abruptly, his eyes narrowed on her.

"I'm no fool, Miss Conover. I realize this book about my mother could be a meal ticket for you. But I won't stand by and watch her open up all those old wounds.''

B.J.'s eyes darkened with anger. In the thin afternoon light spilling through the windows of the foyer, he could see little points of amber flame dance about the pupils.

"It's been—interesting meeting you, Adam. But as I said, this business is really between your mother and me. Or to be more precise, between us and our lawyers and agents."

Then forcing herself to overcome the desire to shout, she hissed, "But if your mother decides to go through with this project, I have no intention of refusing. I'd be a fool to give up a chance like this."

Marching her in silence past the security guard and his bank of monitors, he paused at the front door. The doorman, seeing the anger on their faces, discreetly moved away.

"I doubt we'll have the pleasure of meeting again," Adam said, his tone so low she felt a shiver of apprehension. "I intend to talk some sense into my mother right now. I'm only sorry you came here for nothing."

He held the door and watched as she stepped outside. The biting wind caught her hair, lifting it, flaying it across her cheeks. Turning up the collar of her coat, she cocked her head to one side. Adam London continued to stand in the doorway, looking absolutely formidable despite his injuries.

With a defiant toss of her head, she faced the wind and walked stiffly down the steps.

She turned for one last glimpse of her adversary. The door was closing. She could make out his figure striding purposefully toward the elevator.

Chapter Two

It was snowing, the first real snowfall of the winter. It had begun that morning with big, wet flakes, which had streaked the windows and disappeared on streets and sidewalks. By afternoon, as the temperature dropped, the sky had darkened, and the snow began to stick to cars and buses.

B.J. had the same reaction she always had to the first snowfall. She was a child again, and her steps were lighter and her heartbeat quickened. It was a crazy reaction, she knew. A month from now she would resent the mounds of slush piled at the curb and would join in the chorus of those who moaned about the weather. But right now, this minute, she wanted to run through the streets shouting for joy. Instead, as sedately as she could manage, she paid the cab driver and tipped the doorman to handle the mound of luggage that lay in a heap on the sidewalk. Picking up her briefcase and portable typewriter, she followed him to the elevator that would take her to Nora London's apartment.

It had been two weeks since her initial meeting with the actress. In the interim their lawyers and agents had haggled, and negotiated, and had finally come to a mutual agreement. Contracts were signed that were acceptable to both parties. B.J. knew that it was only a matter of time until her agent got the word to the publishers. Her heart skipped several beats as she realized what she was doing. For the next few months she would step into the fascinating world of a celebrity. She would be privy to long-held secrets. And if everything clicked she would be the author of a best seller.

Nancy Flynn greeted her at the door to the apartment.

"Miss London is resting right now. If you'll follow me, I'll show you to your rooms."

"Thank you." B.J. paused. "Do I call you Nancy?"

"I've been called Flynn for so long, I probably would forget to answer to anything else." Her tone was clipped, her manner distant.

B.J. found herself staring at the jet-black head as she followed the tall figure along the hallway. Not a single hair was out of place. Today, the suit was black, with a simple white blouse, but B.J. knew from the perfectly tailored skirt and jacket that Flynn bought only the best. Nora London was obviously very generous with her staff.

"How long have you worked for Miss London?"

"Twenty-five years."

She stared at the stiff spine. "How old were you when you started?"

"Twenty-three."

B.J.'s mind instantly calculated. "So you're forty-eight now."

The secretary turned. "I'm fifty-three."

"But that doesn't—"

"I left Nora London's employee for five years. Then I came back." The dark eyes dared her to question further. Wordlessly they walked along the hallway, then began to climb a flight of stairs. B.J. expressed amazement at the number of rooms. Flynn haughtily explained that the apartment actually took up the top three floors of the building.

"Miss London and I have private rooms on the lower level. There is a master bedroom, sitting room and small atrium, where Miss London entertains close friends in the afternoon, plus my suite of rooms." As she moved down the hall,

Flynn continued: "On the central level there are a formal living room, dining room, kitchen and library." As she opened the door she added, "On this top level there are two more suites of bedrooms, one for Adam, and this one, which will be yours."

B.J. gasped aloud at the luxury of the rooms that the secretary indicated would be hers. They were like something out of a dream. While the doorman deposited her luggage, she stood in the middle of the room, staring at the elegant surroundings.

The walls were covered with pale ivory chintz. The ivory carpeting was so thick that B.J. knew the minute she was alone she would slip out of her shoes and wriggle her toes in contentment. Along one wall stood a huge bed hung with delicate écru and pink lace draperies at each corner. Matching lace draperies covered the floor-to-ceiling windows that ran the length of one wall. In the corner was a settee covered in delicate pink floral chintz. Two chairs upholstered in pink silk stood on either side. In the center, a mirrored table held a crystal vase of fresh roses. Their scent filled the room.

On the wall opposite the bed was a lovely fireplace of buff brick, with a wide polished oak mantel on which rested a collection of charming crystal animals.

At the sound of a door chime Flynn excused herself. "I'll have someone light a fire. If you need help unpacking, just ring for Gerta. Number four on your telephone. We dine at seven this evening." She turned at the door. "Oh, yes." She glanced disdainfully over the casual attire of her guest. "We dress for dinner."

Of course, mocked B.J. as the door closed. Doesn't everyone? For a moment longer she stared at the door. Where had Nancy Flynn gone for five years? Why had she left, then returned? Her loyalty to Nora London was obvious. But just how far would she go to protect her? B.J. sensed she would get no information from that woman.

She slipped off her shoes and felt her toes sink into the mounds of carpeting. Pulling off the mohair scarf that covered her head, she slipped out of her coat and flung it on a chair. With a toss of her head, she combed her fingers through the tangles and looked around.

Now that she was alone, she felt free to rush from one room to the other, exclaiming over the luxurious appointments. On one side of her bedroom was a sitting room that had obviously been converted to a workroom for her convenience. A seventeenth-century writing table had been positioned in front of the large windows. Beside it was a pair of chaise longues that invited her to stretch out and read in comfort. Along one wall was a Chippendale side table that held an assortment of reference books. Beside it was a typing table and chair. Lifting the cover, B.J. noted the electric typewriter. Miss London, or her secretary, had thought of everything. Through the heavy gauze curtains, B.J. could make out the twinkling lights of the city already coming on in the early dusk.

On the other side of the bedroom was a luxurious bathroom in gold and pink-veined marble. Resting on a silver tray were an assortment of wonderfully scented soaps and vials of creams, lotions and perfumes. B.J. unscrewed the cap of one bottle, sniffed the scent, applied a little, then smiled. Hurriedly spraying an atomizer, she tried another perfume, and then a third and fourth, until, laughing, she twirled happily and stared at her reflection in the full-length mirror. What a thoughtful hostess. Such luxury. She had never known anyone could live such an elegant lifestyle.

With a little laugh, she rushed barefoot into her bedroom, and stopped in mid-stride. Adam London was kneeling by the fireplace, holding a match to some kindling.

As the fire caught he placed several logs over the flame and closed the screen before standing.

Seeing her surprise, he explained, "Sorry. I knocked. I heard something, and thought it was you telling me to come in."

"I was—laughing."

"Yes," he said evenly. "Once inside I recognized the sound. I suppose you have every right to feel smug about your success."

"I was just..." Her smile faded. What was the point of trying to explain to this hostile man? Having lived in such luxury all his life, he wouldn't even begin to understand how she could feel. This was a dream-world. A fairy tale. And for a little while she was going to live in this make-believe palace. But, she thought with a sigh of impatience, looking at his formidable presence, even the princesses of her childhood had to put up with a dragon or two.

She openly stared at the man she had tangled with nearly two weeks before. Adam was now clean-shaven, the bandage removed from his forehead. A thin, dark line revealed the scar that must have been a painful, horrible gash.

Seeing the direction of her gaze, he muttered, "A plastic surgeon will do wonders, I'm told."

"I was thinking that it must have been a frightening thing—to have your Jeep overturn." Her gaze shifted to the arm, still resting in the sling.

He nodded. "Especially since we were under fire from the guerrillas."

B.J. swallowed. "They were shooting at you? I thought the press stayed away from actual combat."

"When we can. This time we were caught in a crossfire. Neither side knew who we..." He stared at her in surprise. "You've known all along who I am, what I do."

Not a question. A statement.

She nodded. "I'd have to live in a cave not to have heard of Adam London. Pulitzer in photojournalism for the picture of an Afghan child last year. A byline in *This Week's News* submitted from all over the globe. Photos of you at plush parties in Monaco, Switzerland. You prefer leggy blondes, I believe."

He gave her a long, silent look.

"When your wounds heal, do you intend to go back?"

Adam shrugged. "Why not? It's my job."

But it doesn't have to be, she thought suddenly. He certainly didn't need the money. It was the danger he craved. The excitement. He was one of those macho types who had to keep proving to himself that he was a man by living on the very edge of disaster. Oh, she knew his type—intimately.

Suddenly she wanted him out of her room, and out of her thoughts.

"Thanks for the fire, Adam. Is there anything else?" She tried to keep the impatience from her tone.

Adam wiped his hand on his pant leg and stared at the figure before him. She stood with her hands on her hips, her chin jutting defiantly. Faded jeans hugged slim, narrow hips and legs. Her feet were bare, nearly buried in the thick carpet. Her hair was a wild tangle of curls that kissed her cheeks and cascaded below her shoulders.

He took several steps past her, then frowned. Sniffing, he said, "You smell like a French..."

He saw her cheeks redden.

"There were so many bottles and atomizers. I—" To hide her embarrassment she laughed self-consciously. "I guess I was like a kid in a candy store. I had to try them all."

She was disarmingly honest. And open. One minute a tomboy in blue jeans. The next, a very sexy woman. With the flush of guilt on her cheeks, she was as appealing as a gamine. He turned away to escape the strong feelings that confused him.

His voice was gruff. "Sorry to have caught you off guard. Flynn got busy elsewhere and asked me to see if you needed anything." He was already moving toward the door.

"Thank you. I have more than I need here. The rooms are wonderful."

"Well—" He turned, with his hand on the knob. "If you need anything, just touch..."

"...four on the phone. Gerta. Flynn told me. Thank you again." She hated to to be rude, but B.J. wanted Adam out of her room. The excitement she had felt just minutes ago was already fading. His presence brought back thoughts long buried. Besides, he made her feel as clumsy as a teenager on her first date.

"Right." He paused, staring intently, until he seemed to realize what he was doing. With more force than necessary, he pulled open the door and strode away.

At precisely seven o'clock B.J. descended the stairs to the dining room. She paused in the doorway to study Nora London, seated on a sunny yellow sofa beside a man with a thatch of white hair.

Was it her imagination, or did the actress look somehow different—thinner, frailer—than she had just two weeks ago?

Adam paused in the act of mixing a drink at the bar to watch the slender figure as she approached. Gone were the casual jeans, the bare feet, the mane of tangles. The woman standing here wore a dress of taupe silk, with matching sandals. Her thick curls were held behind one ear with a jeweled comb. She appeared as poised and sophisticated as any of the women who regularly visited his mother's apartment.

"Oh, Jessica." Nora stood and held out her hand to the young woman. "Come and meet my former agent and dear, dear friend."

As the man stood, Nora beamed. "Martin Stone, this is Bernadette Jessica Conover." With a guileless smile, she added, "Isn't that a lovely name?"

B.J. flinched, causing a smile to cross Adam's face.

"Delightful," Martin muttered, shaking her hand. Peering through thick glasses, he studied B.J. carefully before releasing her hand.

"Nora tells me you're going to write her biography."

As B.J. nodded he said, "You're very lucky, young lady. I never would have believed this if I hadn't heard it from Nora herself."

"Would you like a drink before dinner, Jessica?" Nora asked, deftly changing the subject.

"Yes, thank you. Whatever you're having."

Nora nodded to Adam, who clumsily lifted a bottle with his free hand and poured.

B.J. sat in an eighteenth-century armchair facing the sofa. "Have you known each other a long time?"

Martin smiled and squeezed Nora's arm. The look he bestowed on her was one of real affection.

"We met here in New York, in 1930. Nora was just eighteen then, dancing on stage, and so beautiful, she took my breath away. I went backstage and asked if I could represent her in Hollywood. I'd heard that Josh Thompson was looking for an exotic type for his next picture." Martin laughed. "We all called him 'Mad Thompson.' He was the most imperious, dictatorial man in Hollywood. He drove his cast and crew like a slave-driver. But he was also a genius. He made some of the finest movies ever. They're still regarded as classics."

Beside him Nora smiled and nodded her agreement. "Before my screen test Martin warned me that Josh would drive me to tears. And so he did. But I also discovered a gifted, compulsive man, who was simply driven to be the best."

Adam walked up to hand B.J. a long-stemmed glass of amber wine. As she accepted it their fingers touched. Immediately she glanced up to find his dark gaze centered on her eyes. Nervously licking her lips, she saw his gaze travel over her face and lock on her mouth. Embarrassed, she looked away, resenting the heat that rose to her cheeks.

"Too warm for you, Jess?"

Her head came up sharply at his words. When had he decided to call her that?

"I—yes. It is a bit warm in here." She touched a fingertip to her flaming cheek.

"If you can't stand the heat..."

Her eyes narrowed. He wasn't going to make it easy for her. None of them would.

"I can take it if you can," she challenged.

"Good. This ought to be interesting." He pulled a chair beside hers and sat down, casually crossing one leg over the other.

Setting his drink down on a glass-topped coffee table, he reached into his breast pocket and flipped a cigarette from a pack. Holding a gold lighter to the tip, he inhaled deeply, then released a cloud of smoke. He fumbled for a moment, then replaced the pack and lighter and reached for his drink.

At his frown of impatience his mother laughed. "You're learing to get along nicely with just one good hand."

"Except for the typing," he grumbled.

Martin smiled knowingly. "I don't know why you don't just take these weeks off and rest. Let them find someone else to handle the news until you've completely recovered. All you're doing is adding to your frustration by trying to keep up the work load with that arm in a sling."

"They don't have anyone in the news department who knows that situation over there as intimately as Adam," Nora said calmly. "He's watched the fighting and the political manipulations for almost a year now."

Nora turned to B.J. "Even though Adam's been sidelined for a while, he agreed to continue to interpret the news sent from Central America for his news magazine. The editors need his expertise. Of course," she said with a chuckle, "typewriters were invented for two hands. I'm afraid Adam's quickly losing his patience with the slow recovery process."

"Why don't you hire a typist?" B.J. asked.

"Because I prefer to do it myself." She could hear the exasperation in his tone.

"It just seems the logical solution." She gave an exaggerated shrug. "But I suppose it's just another way to prove to yourself how tough you are."

He raised one eyebrow and seemed primed to respond when Flynn announced, "Dinner is ready."

Martin stood and offered his arm to Nora. Behind them, B.J. walked stiffly beside Adam, feeling his shoulder brush hers as they paused in the doorway.

With a gallant sweep of his hand, he gave her a mocking smile. "Careful. Some guests have been known to eat crow at our table."

Without a word she swept past him and took the seat Nora indicated.

Martin Stone proved to be an entertaining guest. While B.J. relished the Caesar salad and aged prime rib, Martin regaled them with stories about the early days of Hollywood. Throughout his narrative B.J. yearned for a pen and paper. These would make wonderful anecdotes in her novel. He had the rare ability to make that long-ago glamorous era come alive for his listeners.

He turned to Nora. "Do you remember the first time you were introduced to Stephen Hart?"

Nora's eyes lit with the memory. Her lilting laughter joined his.

To B.J. she said, "He bowed grandly and lifted my hand as if to kiss it. Staring deeply into my eyes, he murmured in that marvelous baritone, 'My dear, how fortunate you are to have the privilege of meeting me. Perhaps, if you please me enough, you may even have the privilege of acting with me in a movie.'"

"How did you react?" B.J. asked. She was shocked at the man's vanity.

Again, Nora laughed. "I thought about slapping his face. But I decided that had probably been done—hundreds of times before. So, in my haughtiest tone, I said, 'Oh, I don't think I'd like that, Mr. Hart. The screen isn't big enough for both our egos.'"

"And do you know what he did?" Martin was laughing harder now, remembering the scene.

B.J. shook her head, caught up in their reminiscences.

"For a moment he simply stared at her, with his mouth open in astonishment at her brashness. Everyone around them went silent, waiting for the explosion. Suddenly he burst out laughing. He must have bellowed for several minutes. Wiping tears of laughter from his eyes, he boomed, 'At last, I've found a woman to equal my talents. You, young woman, are going to be my leading lady in my next feature.'"

Recalling the movie history she had studied, B.J. said, "You two went on to become one of the most successful teams in Hollywood. You made four films together, didn't you?"

Nora nodded her head. "And he was so delightful to work with. Actually, that ego thing was all an act for the public. In private he was very sweet. Of course, he did have an eye for the ladies. But every one of his ex-wives continued to be his friend."

B.J. watched Nora's face as she spoke of the infamous actor. Not once did she seem crushed by the memories; her eyes sparkled while she spoke of him. Although the press at the time hinted that he was the father of her child, the reporter in her began to question that rumor. Could Nora London speak so casually about someone who played such a prominent role in her life? Even the finest actress in the world couldn't hide that kind of pain forever. B.J. felt a tiny thrill of excitement at the thought, then dismissed it. Hadn't Nora said his ex-wives and lovers remained his friends?

In time, she knew, Nora London would have to be candid about the affair that rocked Hollywood and ended a fabulous career. The curious would have their answer at last.

"Let's take our coffee in the library," Nora suggested. "Gerta, did you build a fire in there?"

Carrying a tray laden with a silver coffee service, the maid glanced up and nodded, then followed them to the cozy, book-lined room.

As she stood to follow them B.J. was aware of Adam's dark gaze pinning her. It was as if he had read her thoughts and resented her planned intrusion into his life. She shivered at the thought.

B.J. felt her mood lighten as soon as she entered the cheery library. A fire crackled invitingly. Surrounded by leather-bound books, she finally felt truly comfortable in Nora's home. The other luxurious rooms beyond the library walls were alien to her.

Sipping strong coffee, Martin continued his reverie.

"Have you told Jessica about your first reactions to Hollywood?"

Nora shook her head. A dreamy smile played about her lips. To B.J. she explained, "My mother was an early feminist. Of course, in those days, it was called women's suffrage. So I learned to take care of myself at an early age. Mother wanted me to think like a man, and she stressed education and hard work. When Martin sent for me, I took a train from New York. When I arrived in Los Angeles, I hailed a taxi and went to a hotel. Hours later, when we finally located each other, Martin exploded with frustration. He explained that he had arranged for photographers to meet the train. He had intended to hold an impromptu news conference and have all of Hollywood talking about the important New York dancer whose picture was in every newspaper. Instead, seeing the crowd around the station, I slipped out the other way." Nora touched his shoulder in an intimate gesture. "Poor Martin. He was determined to make my name a household word."

"And it happened sooner than we'd hoped," he said, holding a cigar to the flame Adam held out for him. Glancing up, he added, "No matter how hard your mother tried to avoid being a celebrity, it was inevitable. With that face, that figure, and the way she came alive on the screen, she couldn't miss."

B.J. sat near the fireplace, watching the faces of these two friends, and felt a glow of happiness. She had hoped that the woman behind that famous face would turn out to be someone she could like. In order to write an effective biography, she needed to care about the person behind the stories. Nora London, she decided, was a complex, fascinating woman.

The evening passed quickly, with lovely, gentle stories shared by Martin and Nora. B.J. and Adam sat quietly, listening, laughing, and occasionally darting glances at each other.

All too soon Nora and her guest stood to say their goodbyes. Solemnly, Martin took B.J.'s hand and bent low. His words were intended for her ears alone.

"Keep in mind that you're writing about a flesh and blood woman. Nora London was never the celebrity people read about, except in the mind of the press. She was a woman, a very kind, a very good woman. And all too human." His eyes wore a fearful expression. "Don't hurt her."

B.J. met his look. "I'll remember, Martin. Thank you."

As she turned away Adam muttered, "If you really meant that, you wouldn't have come here to write your damned book. When you're finished prying into her life, you can bet she'll be hurt."

"I won't dignify that with a response. But try to remember that I'm here at your mother's invitation. This book was her idea." Too angry to say more, she turned stiffly away.

After saying good night to the others, B.J. climbed the stairs to her rooms. As soon as she was alone the weariness, the confusion and the anger she had felt downstairs with Adam left her. Her elegant surroundings reminded her of the new world she had entered and all she still had to discover.

Quickly removing her clothes, she slipped into a long silk robe and began to jot notes for herself. In her eagerness she grabbed the first thing available. On the back of a book of matches, she wrote the names of the director and actors Martin Stone had mentioned earlier. She tore a page from a frayed notebook and began to jot little items she wanted to remember—dates, events, anecdotes. Finally, convinced that she had covered everything, she stacked the notes on her dresser for future reference and flexed her cramped fingers.

Standing, she stretched lazily, like a cat. She strode to the wall of glass, and opened the drapes to stare at the lights of the city, spread out like a million tiny diamonds below. Newly fallen snow frosted the floor and railing of the balcony outside her room.

"Oh." With a little gasp of pleasure, B.J. threw open the door and stepped into the crisp night air. "It's magic! The whole world looks new." Holding her arms wide, B.J. lifted her face to catch the snowflakes that still fell silently in the darkness.

Far below, the traffic sounds were muted in the thick snow. The lights were a hazy glow. Suddenly B.J. grabbed a handful of snow, formed a snowball, and tossed it into the darkness. A low, throaty chuckle bubbled from her lips. A snowball fight. That's what she wanted. And Adam London would be the imaginary target. Hurriedly she packed the snow into a ball, eager to hurl it.

A sudden flash of light behind her caused her to turn. Adam was clad in a pair of faded khaki pants that rode low on his hips. A heavy flannel shirt covered his chest and one arm. An empty sleeve hung limply, and the front of the shirt bulged over the plaster cast. As he snapped the lighter shut, a curl of smoke drifted above his head. The scent of tobacco wafted on the air.

"How did you get here?" The moment the words were out of her mouth, she realized how silly they sounded.

One glance showed her that the balcony wrapped around the entire side of the building. It was as accessible to Adam's room as it was to hers.

"I walked. How did you get here, fly?" He stood, ankle deep in the snow, leaning casually against the rough concrete of the building.

"I wasn't aware that the balcony was so big. I thought it was only outside my room."

"Do you always run around in the snow dressed like that?"

She glanced down at the hem of her pale robe. It trailed damply in the snow. Turning her back on him, she again lifted her face to the sky. "I've always loved the first snowfall. I had to come out here. There's something so—special about it."

"Magic, I believe you said."

She turned slightly, to study his dour expression. "Do you always make it a point to spy on guests?"

"Now, that takes real nerve. You, calling me a spy."

Too angry to think, B.J. picked up a handful of snow. With no thought to what she was doing, she reflexively tossed it at Adam. It caught him in the face. There was a moment of shocked silence in which B.J. could only stare at him in horror.

He tossed aside his cigarette and moved menacingly nearer. "So you want to play in the snow, do you?"

With one hand he scooped up the snow from the railing and washed her face. Outraged, she retaliated by flinging snow in his hair. He caught at her hand, but she slipped from his grasp and turned, quickly packing a snowball and pitching it with deadly accuracy. It caught him on the side of the head.

Wiping away the last traces, he caught her arm before she could throw a second one. She nearly pulled free, but the hand gripping her arm was too strong. With no effort he hauled her against him. Through the delicate fabric of her robe, she could feel the warmth of his body, and to one side, the outline of the rough plaster cast.

Looking down at her, he saw the gleam of mischief in her eyes. Damn her! What kind of woman could be desirable while still managing to be so infuriating? He wondered if she had any idea how appealing she looked. Her cheeks were as red as autumn apples. Her eyelashes were matted. Her hair was a wild tangle. Snowflakes adorned her hair like tiny jewels.

"You thought you had the advantage because I have only one good arm." His tone was low, angry.

"I'll take any advantage I can." Her breath was coming in short gasps, making her voice even more husky.

"Then be warned. So will I." The arm holding her against him tightened perceptibly. He inhaled the delicate fragrance of her.

His face lowered. She stared into those gray eyes and saw them narrow slightly. His fingers twined through the hair that cascaded down her back. A tremor flickered through her at his touch, and she fought to ignore it. She could feel the imprint of his thighs pressed tightly to hers. For one long, pulsing moment, his lips hovered just above hers. Her heart hammered in her throat. Anticipation shivered through her. Feeling her tremble, he stepped back a pace.

"You'd better get inside before you freeze to death."

"Yes." She swallowed and nearly stumbled.

Catching her arm, he steadied her a moment, then stepped back abruptly. His voice was mocking. "It's going to be a long, cold winter, Jess. Maybe we can play in the snow another time."

"Find yourself another playmate." She flung the words, turning away.

"What's the matter, Jess? Do I play too rough?" His tone was low, taunting.

She felt her fury rising. He was pompous, conceited and so damned sure of himself.

"No. You want to play hardball, Adam. I do that in my work. But when I play, I like to have fun."

As she started through the doorway of her room, he caught her arm roughly and spun her around. "So it's fun you want." His dark gaze traveled over her features. "Then maybe you'll enjoy this." His mouth covered hers in a hard, bruising kiss.

Shocked, B.J. had no time to resist. In those first moments she stood motionless, experiencing sensations that rocked her. Then she became caught up in the kiss, enjoying the softness of his lips, aware of the slight tang of brandy and tobacco in his taste.

Adam London was an expert in the art of seduction. His lips moved over hers gently, exploring, tasting. When she began to relax in his embrace, the kiss became more demanding, the arm around her tightened, drawing her even closer to him. Without realizing it, her arms went around his waist, clinging to his strength. She opened her lips for his further exploration. His tongue, his lips, took her higher.

When he had explored her mouth at leisure, he lifted his head. Slowly, she opened her eyes.

He smiled, enjoying the look of confusion on her face.

"That wasn't bad," he murmured. "We'll have to do this again some time. You can write it off to research."

Hot, blazing anger replaced all other emotions. Giving him a hate-filled look, she snapped, "Why you pompous, egotistical...there won't be another time."

"You're going to be here for weeks, Jess. Months, maybe. Want to bet there'll be a next time?"

"You keep away from me, Adam. Do you hear?"

He grinned. "Or what? You'll run and tell my mother?"

"Oh, don't worry. I can take care of myself. I've been doing it for a long time now."

With his low rumble of laughter mocking her, she turned away and slammed the door. As she drew the drapes she could see him still standing on the balcony, staring at the lights of New York.

Adam shook another cigarette from his pack and lit it. As he blew out the smoke he frowned in the darkness. That kiss had caught him by surprise. And yet, it shouldn't have. He had found himself thinking about her ever since that first time they met. He could still remember the silky feel of her hair. He'd been curious to see if her lips would be soft, yielding. Maybe it was the fiery temper to match that hair. Or the humor and honesty in her eyes. Yes, maybe it was those intriguing green eyes.

He flicked the cigarette over the balcony and walked to his room. Maybe it had just been too quiet and serene since he'd returned home. After Central America, he needed something stimulating. This could be their own private, intimate little war.

Oh, yes, Bernadette Jessica Conover, he thought with a smile. There'd be another time. Another battle of wills. And he intended to win every one.

Chapter Three

The snow had stopped sometime during the night. The sun rose, brilliantly reflecting off a land transformed into a frozen fairyland. Through the gauzy drapes, B.J. watched the dazzling display of sun dancing on fresh snowfall. Her first conscious thoughts were of Adam. How could she manage to live and work here, under the watchful eye of a man who aroused such strong feelings in her?

Last night she had lain awake, puzzling over the powerful emotions unleashed when Adam had kissed her. She had sensed the pull of that man from the first moment she had been introduced to him, but she had never dreamed that a simple kiss could arouse her like that. Now, more than ever, she would have to keep out of his way.

Forcing herself into action, she rose from the comfortable bed. From her balcony B.J. could see the traffic snarled far below. She was grateful she didn't have to be out in it. Shivering, she pulled on warm slacks and a cheery red angora sweater.

If this were her own apartment, she would plug in the coffee maker and sit crosslegged on the floor to read the morning paper. She could get in two or three strong cups of caffeine to stimulate her brain and put her in the right frame of mind to cope with the day. But remembering where she was, B.J. ran a brush through her hair, applied makeup, and slipped her feet into shoes before leaving the room. She wondered how many other concessions she would make before this project ended.

Last night, just as she was falling asleep, she had heard the sound of typing. It had sounded very close, but sleep had overtaken her before she had a chance to sort it out in her mind. It was odd, she thought, passing Adam's room, that his typing could be heard clear into her bedroom.

Breakfast, B.J. was to discover, was as simple a morning ritual in the world of a celebrity as it was anywhere else. The only difference was, someone else made the coffee.

In the dining room Adam looked up from the morning paper. Clad in faded jeans and a shirt that had been buttoned crookedly over the plaster cast, he looked as rumpled as she felt. His feet were bare. Under his lower lip, two stained bits of tissue stuck to his chin.

The best way to avoid mentioning that scene last night was to attack. "You have something on your face," she said.

"I know. I cut myself shaving." Leaning his broken arm heavily on the paper, he folded it, shook it, then lifted it in his good hand. "So many things are really hard to do with one hand."

"Umm. You could grow a beard to save time."

"That's what I do when I'm off on assignment. Then, each time I return to civilization, I have to learn to shave all over again."

Her tone was mocking, remembering their encounter in the snow. "You call this returning to civilization? I thought you were still engaged in jungle warfare." Annoyed at the slip of her tongue, B.J. turned to the silver coffeepot and poured herself a cup. With a glance at the uncomfortable looking sling, she asked, "Want some?"

"Thanks." He set down the paper and held out his cup. His eyes glittered with humor at her bad temper. "Of course, there are still plenty of things I can manage one-handed. Pouring a drink, throwing a snowball." His tone softened. "Holding a woman..."

"Cute, Adam." She picked up the other half of the paper and tried to ignore him.

He studied the turned-up nose, the thrust of her chin. How could she manage to look so fresh and appealing at this ungodly hour?

Gerta entered with freshly squeezed orange juice. "What would you like for breakfast, Miss Jessica?" The accent was German; her manner of speech with this intruder formal.

"Nothing, thanks. Just coffee. Gallons of it."

A few minutes later the maid returned with a plate of steaming sausages, eggs, toast and jelly for Adam. B.J. watched him in silence for several seconds, then lifted her paper higher to avoid seeing his amused smile. The aroma of the spicy sausages made her mouth water. She couldn't remember the last time she had bothered to eat breakfast. The thought of that steaming plate of food was driving her crazy.

"Would you like a taste?"

She lowered the paper. "No, thank you."

The warmth of unspoken laughter colored his tone. "Speaking of taste. Last night, you tasted like lemon ice. Tart and sweet at the same time. In fact, I think that's a good description of you."

Her face flushed. "Careful, Adam. You're treading on thin ice." She ducked behind the newspaper.

With a grin, he said, "The sausages are great. Sure you wouldn't like a little bite?"

"No."

"I hate to eat alone. Try it."

She sighed, as if in defeat. "If I take a bite, will you stop badgering me? I really can't stand to make conversation until I've been up for at least an hour."

"Promise." Adam held the fork to her mouth.

"Thank you."

"Want Gerta to fix you some? It's a great way to start the day."

She yielded to the teasing laughter in his eyes. "All right. I guess I could try to eat a little."

"Great." He grinned, and she felt her heart do a somersault. "Gerta."

A moment later the plump woman entered from the kitchen.

"Yes?"

"Miss Conover has changed her mind." He gave B.J. a knowing look. "As women often do. She'll have what I'm having."

The maid's face was impassive. With a curt nod, she was gone.

"Will your mother and Flynn be joining us?" Maybe this would be a safe topic.

"Mother is probably having coffee and juice up in her bedroom, accompanied by several daily newspapers. She's a compulsive reader. And Flynn is never seen before noon, unless there's been a world crisis. She breakfasts alone in her room, and then meets with Mother to go over the day's schedule.''

Gerta returned with a steaming plate of eggs and sausage, toast and jelly. Pouring more coffee, she asked, ''Will there be anything else?'' Though her face didn't betray her emotions, whenever she spoke to B.J. her tone was frosty.

''Nothing, thanks.''

With a warm smile for Adam, the maid silently left the room.

Stirring cream into her coffee, B.J. mused that she would get no cooperation from the people around Nora London. Her secretary, maid, and especially her son couldn't be counted on for information. But at least, she thought with a sigh, the schedule around here would be very compatible with her own work habits. Her mornings would be left free to research or write. In the afternoon she would probably meet with the actress, to record anything she thought important enough to be included in her biography. And after dinner B.J. could again work on her manuscript until it was time for bed. Her work would also give her an excuse to slip away immediately after dinner each evening, thus avoiding Adam. With enthusiasm, she dug into the hearty breakfast.

When she set down her newspaper, Adam took it in exchange for the section he had already read. Automatically picking up the part he discarded, she devoured the morning news. They ate and read in companionable silence, each uncomfortably aware of the other, each trying to hide it.

"More coffee?"

"Ummm. Thanks." She barely glanced up.

As Adam picked up her cup he leaned close, inhaling the delicate lemon fragrance of shampoo that lingered in her hair. He could still remember the way she felt last night, warm and pliant against him. He fought the swift rush of desire that left him slightly shaken.

As he sat back down he watched the morning sunlight play among the strands of her hair. What a picture she made. Slipping one foot beneath her, she turned the pages of the newspaper, completely absorbed in her reading. She was an artless beauty. It was a shame, he thought, that she had to be the enemy. Under more pleasant circumstances he would have enjoyed her company. As it was, he would have to be careful to remind himself what she was doing here.

She glanced up to catch him staring at her.

"You have an interesting face," he murmured. "I'd like to photograph you, Jess."

Taken by surprise, she felt the heat stain her cheeks. Composing herself, she said with disdain, "Save it for some stagestruck ingenue, Adam. I'm sure there are plenty of them here in New York, just waiting for their big break. I'll bet that line gets you a lot of mileage."

He grinned wickedly. "You can't blame a guy for trying."

Quickly changing the subject, she stood. "I have work to do. But don't think this hasn't been enlightening."

As she walked away Adam watched her with an admiring glance. As long as he held her at arm's length, he could enjoy engaging the enemy. He could hardly wait for their next sparring match.

In her room B.J. kicked off her shoes and picked up the stack of notes on her dresser. The first order of business was to put them in some sort of logical sequence. Then maybe she'd type an outline of the questions she'd like to ask Nora about her early years. The actress had mentioned that her mother was a pioneering feminist. That ought to be interesting.

B.J. bit her lip, thinking about her own mother. They had moved so many times, the towns were just a blur in her memory. And each time her mother had stoically set about trying to turn one of those drab apartments near the military base into a home.

B.J. could remember little about her father. He always seemed to be in uniform. He was always leaving for another important mission. He'd been a big man; big hands, big, hearty laugh. Her mother's face seemed lit by some inner radiance each time he walked through the door. It was as if their lives were suspended, a joyless, colorless gray, until he arrived to bring them back their sparkle, their purpose.

Then one day he went off to war and never returned. Her mother then seemed to exist in some kind of limbo, remembering all the things they had done, the places they had been together. B.J. thought of her mother's little house, now occupied by an aging aunt. It nestled beside rows of other little houses, all neat and tidy, all looking the same. Her father's picture smiled down from the mantel, beside a portrait of her mother. B. J. frowned. Her mother had built her entire life around a man who was more interested in the thrill of danger than in making a home for them.

For long moments B.J. stared at the wall, seeing nothing. She had never forgiven her father for not coming back. He had taken the light out of her mother's eyes forever. He had abandoned her— abandoned them both.

With an angry stab of her pen, she made some final notes, then closed her notebook.

Again she heard the sound of typing. Walking to the door of the sitting room, she saw Adam at the typing table in her workroom.

"What are you doing here?"

"Isn't it obvious?" He flipped a page of handwritten notes and continued pecking at the keys with one hand.

"But I thought this was my workroom. I didn't realize we'd be sharing it."

He glanced up. "It's a big room, Jess. We can manage not to step on each other."

Can we? she wondered. Studying his figure huddled over the typewriter, she felt her earlier elation ebbing. How could she work with Adam here? How could she concentrate, knowing how he felt about her proposed biography of his mother?

Looking at the boudoir lounges, she felt a stab of regret. She had envisioned herself reclining there in comfort like a model in one of those magazines. How could she possibly lie there, poring over the secrets of someone he loved, and pretend that he wasn't involved in it? This was going to be an awkward situation.

She carried in the assorted scraps of paper and notes and set them on the writing table in front of the window. Since Adam was using the electric typewriter and Chippendale side table for his work, she would use this side of the room for hers. As silently as possible she went back to her bedroom for the portable typewriter she had brought with her.

When she returned, Adam was standing beside her desk, looking down at the jumble of notes.

"What's all that?"

She glowered. "They're notes I made last night. Names, dates. Martin Stone's stories were so appealing, I decided I may want to use them in the biography.''

He pointed to the matchbook. "More notes?"

She turned it over to reveal her handwriting. "It was the first thing available. I was in a hurry."

"Very professional, Jess." He sauntered back to his typing table.

Fuming, B.J. set up her typewriter and began an outline of the work she wanted to cover this afternoon.

They worked for nearly two hours. The silence was punctuated by the steady beat of her typewriter keys, and the uneven sound of Adam, pecking awkwardly. At least once every five minutes or so, Adam swore, ripped a page from the machine, and clumsily inserted another. B.J. suppressed a laugh as the floor became littered with balled papers.

When her work was completed, she walked past him toward the door of her bedroom. Adam let loose with stream of curses as he tore another sheet of paper from the typewriter and hurled it aside.

She stopped. With her hand on her hip, she surveyed the litter, then clucked, "Very professional, Adam."

Quickly closing the door, she grinned as he let loose with another torrent of swearing.

A few minutes later Adam pounded on her door and called, "Jess, Flynn's out here. She wants to talk to you."

B.J. opened the door. Ignoring Adam, she smiled at the secretary. "Is Miss London ready to see me?"

Flynn glanced at the floor. "I'm afraid she isn't up to seeing you today. She sent word that she'd like to postpone the first session until tomorrow."

B.J.'s heart fell. She didn't like the sound of it. Was the actress having second thoughts about the project? Last night she had been at her charming best. Why this sudden delay?

"Well, maybe we can talk at dinner."

"Miss London is having dinner out this evening. She wants you and Adam to let Gerta know what time you'd like to eat."

Glancing at Adam, seated once more at the typewriter, B.J. made up her mind quickly. There was nothing more she could do here today. She might as well enjoy this unexpected day off.

"I won't be eating here tonight, Flynn. As long as I can't see Miss London, I think I'll take a hike through Central Park. All that snow is too tempting to resist."

When the secretary walked away, B.J. hurriedly closed the door. After pulling on a pair of sturdy boots, she grabbed her coat, a warm scarf, and a pair of gloves, and headed for the elevator.

The streets of New York were a symphony of sound. Cars and taxis blared their horns, venting their impatience with traffic snarled in the fresh snow. Sirens wailed, adding a mournful note to the music. Pedestrians slogged through the snow, their faces ruddy from the exertion. Heat from doorways mingled with steam from sewers and exhaust fumes from stalled traffic.

Through it all, B.J. smiled, loving the sights and sounds of this city. If she couldn't be lying in a hammock in the sun, she thought, there was no place she'd rather be than right here. She thrived on the chaos.

She leaped over a mound of snow at the curb and crossed the street, then walked slowly along the almost-deserted walk leading into the park. At every corner she stopped to watch the squirrels, hastily gathering scraps of food, nuts and berries, then scurrying back to the warmth of their nests.

Perched on a rock, she fed peanuts to a bold chipmunk. "Didn't your mother teach you about hibernation?" she chided him.

Adam's jacket hung open. It was impossible to button it over the bulk of the cast. He was not, he told himself as he turned down another lane of Central Park, looking for Jess. He just craved fresh air.

Ahead of him, the figure in the camel coat paused, and he increased his speed, hoping to catch up with her. As he reached her side she turned, and he felt a stab of disappointment. The hair beneath the scarf was faded blond, not fiery.

The eyes were gray, not green. She gave him a startled look as he stared at her, mumbled a greeting, then hurried on.

He passed Tavern on the Green and looked up at the raucous sound of a group of partygoers climbing into horse-drawn carriages. Pulling up his collar, he hurried on. With his head bent against the wind, he passed the figure on the rock. The husky sound of her laughter caused him to stop in his tracks. Peering through the gathering dusk, he retraced his steps. Tossing another peanut, she laughed at the antics of her new friend.

"Does he do any tricks?"

She looked up sharply, then relaxed at the sight of Adam.

"He's been stuffing himself for over an hour. It must mean it's going to be a long winter."

"Or it could mean he just likes to hoard food."

"That could be it. I don't know where he's putting it all."

"Probably dropping it under a nearby rock. When you leave, he'll haul it all home to the wife and kids."

"Here." She dropped several peanuts into Adam's hand as he sat down beside her on the rock. "See if he'll take them from you."

Perplexed, the little chipmunk refused to come near the big hand that reached out toward him. Even the scent of food couldn't entice him to come closer.

B.J. shook the last of her peanuts in the snow and stood. "I should have known."

"Known what?"

"My friend here is probably warning me. He senses that you're not to be trusted."

"Sound advice. Any time a chipmunk tells you something, you ought to listen."

They watched as the horse-drawn carriages drew alongside them. The horses' hooves were muted in the snow. The sound of laughing voices trailed on the air as the carriages vanished around a bend in the road.

Near the entrance to the park they stopped at a hot-dog vendor.

"Had dinner yet?" Adam asked.

"No. I forgot to eat."

"We'll have to do something about that. Come on. I'll treat."

"Thanks, big spender."

Laughing, B.J. balanced two foot-long hot dogs, smothered in onions and mustard, and two cups of steaming coffee, while Adam paid the man. Brushing the snow from a park bench, they sat and ate while throngs of people rushed by.

"Umm. That was so good."

"Could you eat another?"

"I'll eat half if you'll eat the other half."

"You're on." Adam bought another hot dog and gave it to her to break into two. Laughing like two children, they finished every bite.

Wiping mustard from her lips, B.J. sighed in contentment.

Replete, Adam stretched his arm along the back of the park bench and leaned back, watching her. Her cheeks were flushed from the cold. Her eyes sparkled as she studied the throngs of people hurrying past. He couldn't remember the last time he'd laughed so easily with a woman.

"What makes you want to get inside people's lives, Jess?"

She looked away. "I don't know. I've always wanted to know what makes them tick. I'm fascinated by why people do the things they do. Why does a hero risk his life? Because he has less fear than other men, or because he just happens to be in the wrong place at the wrong time?" She turned to glance up at his puzzled look. "Why does a man kill and even take his own life, over a selfish, unfaithful woman?" Her voice lowered. "For that matter, why does a woman throw away everything she's worked for, for a moment's pleasure?"

The image of Nora London flashed into both their minds.

His eyes narrowed. His hand tightened into a fist. "You never let go, do you, Jess?"

"It's what I do, Adam. I research. I write. Tell me why you keep going off to those dirty little wars."

He met the challenge in her eyes. "You think I go there for the glory?"

"Are you telling me you like hearing guns in the night? Do you like watching people kill?"

"Come on, Jess. You know better than that."

"Do I? You tell me, Adam. Why do you keep going back? Isn't it because you want to prove what a brave man you are? Does't something inside you drive you to live always on the edge of danger?"

He watched the change in her. It started in her voice. No longer just curious, her tone was accusing. And then in her eyes. They flashed with anger. The green darkened. Little points of flame challenged him.

"Why does my job threaten you, Jess?"

She blinked. Lowering her head, she said, "I really don't care what you do, Adam. It's none of my concern."

Standing, she began furiously brushing the snow from her clothes. Adam stood and caught her hand, stopping her movements. Startled, she stared up into the cold steel of his gaze.

"You resent what I do. And yet we're both investigative reporters. We just choose to deal with very different topics. Why this anger, Jess?"

"I hate all those dirty little wars." He heard a tremble in her voice.

"And you think I don't?"

"I think"—she paused, licking her lips—"I think you glorify them."

"Glorify!" With his good hand, he caught her by the shoulder, roughly shaking her. "Did you think that photo of a little Afghan child with no arms glorified war? Do you think the flattened villages, the wounded and dead victims, the grieving survivors glorify war? My God! It's ugly. Vicious. I'd like nothing better than to have no more war to report on. But until that day I'll go on doing what I do best."

She pulled her arm roughly from his grip and stepped back a pace. "And go on proving how tough you are."

She turned and began trudging through the snow. For long moments he simply stared at her. Then, his carefully controlled anger erupting, he strode after her and caught her, spinning her around.

"What's really eating at you, Jess?"

"You! Keep away from me, Adam. Just leave me alone to do my job."

"I'll be more than happy to leave you alone. The only problem is, you intend to expose my mother, and the events of my birth, for the entire world's entertainment. Do you expect me to just stand by and enjoy it?"

"I don't care what you do, Adam. Just leave me alone."

B.J. twisted from his grip and managed nearly three steps before slipping on a patch of ice. With a little gasp, she fell in the snow.

His strong hand caught her. Lifting her easily to her feet, Adam asked, "Are you all right?"

Wide eyes met his. She took a deep breath. "Yes. I'm fine. Just startled."

He continued to hold her. "Are you sure you haven't twisted an ankle? I could carry you."

"With one arm? Even you aren't that strong. No." She tested her weight on the other foot. "I'm fine."

Still, he continued to hold her. She tensed.

"Last night, when you were throwing those snowballs, you were really mad, weren't you, Jess?"

Her eyes rounded. "What's that?"...

"Weren't you?"

"Yes."

"And right now. You're mad again, aren't you?"

"What're you getting at?"

"Yes or no?"

"Yes," she hissed. "I'm mad enough to kick you in the ankle if you don't let me go, Adam."

"I thought so." He grinned.

B.J. felt a thread of alarm. His smile was almost as dangerous as his frown.

"Last night I told myself that if I ever kissed you again, I'd keep on kissing you until your knees buckled."

"Adam, so help me—"

"Why don't you stop me, Jess?"

His lips brushed softly over hers. She stiffened, and tried to pull back. His hand tightened at her shoulder, holding her firmly against him. Before she could react, his lips covered hers. He could feel her heartbeat hammering in her chest. Her fingers curled into this shirt. With a little sigh, she gave herself up to the kiss.

With a will of their own, her arms went around his waist. Drawing her more firmly to him, he lifted his head to change the angle of the kiss. Bathed in a pool of lamplight, he studied her eyes, green and glowing. Then his lips once more covered hers. Desire blazed between them.

B.J. was aware of his lean strength. As he bent toward her his hair fell over his forehead like black silk. She was aware of the musky male scent of him. Taking the kiss deeper, she tasted all the dark secrets of his mouth.

Her anger had completely disappeared. Now there was only this wonderful pleasure that his touch, his kiss offered. Giving herself up to it, she drew herself closer to him, as her body became a mass of nerve endings.

Adam had anticipated the excitement that sparked whenever they came together. He had hoped for more of the simmering passion he had sensed in her last night. What he hadn't expected was the need. Raw and desperate, it drove him deeper into the kiss.

With a little moan, he lifted his lips from hers and buried them in the hollow of her throat. Arching her neck, she reveled in the delightful tremors that his lips brought.

He felt a flash of frustration at the awkwardness of having only one hand. He wanted to hold her, feel her, with every part of his body. The plaster cast was a barrier.

Beneath her coat, his hand roamed from the flare of her hip, to the slender waist, then upward to the soft swell of her breast. He was losing himself to the surging, compelling need for this woman. As his thumb continued stroking, his lips again found her mouth, warm and willing.

He had to end this, and yet he had to have her. The need for her rocked him. He hadn't wanted this driving hunger. He had wanted only to kiss her until she was soft and pliant in his arms. He had wanted to tease her, to taunt. Only now his needs taunted him. Slowly releasing her, he stepped back and looked at her.

Both of them had been shattered by this contact. Neither of them was willing to admit it.

Struggling for breath, B.J. took in long gulps of air and stood very straight. She could still feel the imprint of his body on hers, the touch of his fingers on her skin.

Adam jammed his hand in his pocket in a casual pose. His voice, when he finally spoke, was a low rasp.

"I'll stay out of your way as long as you stay out of mine." When she didn't speak, he turned. "Come on. I'll walk you back to make sure you don't fall again."

He was careful not to touch her. He didn't want her to see that his hand was shaking.

Chapter Four

For long moments she simply stared at him, unable to speak. Then she moved mechanically alongside him, careful not to touch him. A moment ago she had been on fire. Now she trembled against the night chill.

B.J. was a woman, with a woman's needs. She understood passion, desire. But this hunger was something new. For the first time in her life something had taken control of her that she couldn't fathom. She was a logical person. She relished researching, sifting through information, discovering all the reasons for a person's behavior.

Was Adam playing with her emotions? Was this his way of getting back at her for meddling in his life?

She lifted her head and cast a quick glance at his profile. Sensing her look, he turned to her in the gathering darkness. The need throbbed through her again, shocking her with its intensity.

Why now, with this man? B.J. prided herself on being able to handle men. There had been other men in her life, and there were many men she considered friends. But the minute she sensed that they wanted more than friendship, she held them at a distance. There was no room in her life yet for marriage, children. That had been her mother's only goal in life. And look where it had taken her.

Someday, B.J. thought, there will be time for that. I really want it all. Career. Husband. Family. But right now it takes all my energy to work. The rest will have to wait. She was surprised at the swift surge of pain that followed on the heels of that thought. Until now she had always been so sure of her goals.

They swept past the doorman and into the heated foyer, past the security guard and his bank of monitors. Adam punched the elevator button, and they stood in silence, each acutely aware of the other. She could feel the frustration in him, the anger, and was reminded of the first time she had met him. As they entered the apartment B.J. saw a flash of color in the hallway.

"Your mother hasn't gone out yet?" she asked.

Adam shrugged. "It's probably Flynn."

Drab, colorless Flynn? B.J. nearly laughed.

From a room on the lower level came the sound of classical music. Following the sound, Adam and B.J. stopped in the doorway of the secretary's suite of rooms.

Flynn, a long-stemmed glass of wine in her hand, swayed softly to the music. The black hair, always tightly bound, fell in soft waves to her shoulders. She was wearing an elegant caftan of brilliant pinks and purples, shot with gold thread.

Hearing their footsteps, she turned. "Oh, you're back." Her voice sounded dreamy. "Your mother is out for the evening. I hope you ate."

Adam gave her a gentle smile. "Yes. We're fine. Thanks, Flynn. Expecting company?"

She nodded.

"Enjoy yourself."

Touching B.J.'s elbow, he urged her along the hall.

At her door B.J. paused and met his eyes. "I wouldn't have believed it if I hadn't actually seen it. Does the wren often become a peacock?"

"Flynn works hard for my mother. What she does after hours is her business."

"But she's—stunning. Why is she hiding it all behind that prim hairstyle and those matronly suits?"

"You'll have to ask her." Without realizing it, Adam caught a strand of her hair and wound it around his finger. His eyes narrowed. "You're stunning too."

"Don't, Adam."

"Don't what?"

She tried to pull her head back, but he continued to hold her by the strand of hair.

"Don't start that again." Her eyes darkened in the light of the hallway. "You know it's a dead end."

"Is it?" He drew her closer. His gaze centered on her mouth, then moved upward to her eyes. "I think, Jess, that you and I have a long way to go. I don't think either of us is going to be satisfied with just a kiss."

His mouth hovered above hers, his breath mingling with hers as she sought to control the little tremor that shivered through her at his words.

"Then I have the perfect solution. Don't bother kissing me again."

His hand slid around her neck, catching a tangle of hair. His voice, low, seductive, sent heat surging through her veins. He saw her eyelids flutter, as if in anticipation of his kiss.

"I have a much better solution, Jess. One that would satisfy both our hungers."

Her eyes opened wide. He saw the flash of fire in their depths and smiled. "Better lock your door."

Before she could respond, he dropped his hand and walked away. With more force than necessary, she slammed her door shut.

He heard the lock turn. With a glint of humor he strode to his room.

"I've been rambling for hours. Are you getting tired?"

B.J. looked up from her notebook. "Not at all. I'm fascinated."

"Is there anything special you'd like me to talk about now?"

"Why don't you tell me about your parents."

The actress stiffened for a moment, but B.J., turning the page of her tablet, failed to notice. She and Nora were comfortably ensconced in the atrium, a lovely, plant-filled sitting room on the lower level of the apartment. They had been talking quietly for over two hours, Nora rambling about anything that interested her, B.J. scribbling copious notes.

The older woman's voice softened. "My mother divorced my father when I was three. I don't remember him at all. I think I once mentioned that my mother was a suffragette. Most of my memories are of her fighting for a cause."

Nora gave B.J. a smile. "Mother was such a firebrand. I can still see her, emotional, arguing with anyone willing to listen, or worse, fight back.

She was never content with the status quo. Always trying to change the world.''

''What did she think of her daughter eventually making her living as a dancer?'' B.J.'s pen poised above the paper.

For long moments Nora studied the pattern on the cushion beside her. ''She expected me to earn my own way. How I did it was my business. The truth is, I think my mother was too wrapped up in her own world to even notice.''

''Did she ever tell you about your father?''

Again, B.J. noted the softer tone of the actress, as if to cushion the pain.

''Only when I asked a specific question. I don't recall my mother ever volunteering any information about him. I did learn that he was very young when they married. She was twenty-nine and he was only twenty. He left his father's farm in the Midwest for the lights of New York. He held a succession of odd jobs. I never knew if he deserted us because he couldn't make a go of it in the big city, or if my mother's''—she paused a moment, then plunged ahead—''overzealous nature drove him away.''

Something in B.J. responded to the note of sadness in Nora's tone. She realized how difficult it was for the actress to discuss those early years. Yet B.J. forced herself to ask the tough question that begged an answer.

"In all those years Adam was growing up, didn't you sometimes feel that history was repeating itself?"

"I never saw it that way. I tried to give my son as much of my time as he needed. I struggled to give him a normal home life." Her voice lowered. "At least as normal as life could be with photographers dogging my footsteps each time I left the apartment and reporters writing about every man I ever spoke to. I think I was a good mother. Despite the difficulties, we were very happy."

B.J.'s glance centered on a priceless crystal sculpture resting on the table beside a bowl of orchids. "You left New York at the age of eighteen, earning a dancer's pay. After thirteen films in Hollywood, you retired. You obviously didn't marry and divorce several millionaires. Yet, if this apartment is a fair indication of your lifestyle, you've never wanted for money. Where does it come from?"

The actress leaned forward, her eyes suddenly alert. This was a comfortable topic for discussion.

"When I signed my first movie contract, I set aside enough money to make a down payment on a lovely house. That was something I did just for me. To fill a need. A real home. Then I began buying up the property nearby. Next I hired the best investment counselor in California. I told him to draw up a comprehensive plan, covering short- and long-term investments. I explained that within fifteen years, I intended to have my future as secure as humanly possible."

"And what did you finally invest in?"

Blue eyes danced with confidence. "Against all advice, I stayed with land."

B.J. tapped her pen on her notebook. "Land?"

The actress sat back with an air of confidence. "At one time I owned some of the most expensive real estate in California."

This cool, logical, business side of the actress's nature surprised B.J. She had somehow thought of her as a dreamy, artistic woman who had made money from her films, and then, forced by unfortunate circumstances to flee Hollywood, had simply lived on her savings. B.J. had even assumed that Adam's father had contributed something, either annually, or in a lump-sum settlement. But no mention had been made of him at all. It was as though he never existed.

"I could have been a successful businesswoman." Nora's eyes danced. "I used to envision myself running a financial empire. But men never wanted to take me seriously."

B.J. studied the famous face. Had she resented her fame? Had the price been too great?

Both women glanced up at a knock on the door. Adam paused in the doorway.

"I'm sorry to disturb your work. Flynn asked me to find you, Mother. Martin's on the phone. Claims he needs to talk to you now."

The actress sighed. "Thanks, Adam." With a smile at B.J. she said, "I suppose I've given you enough for today anyway." Rising, she noted B.J.'s questioning look and asked, "One final question?"

"When you hired the investment counselor, why did you set a limit of fifteen years?"

Nora sank back down. "I was eighteen years old when I arrived in Hollywood. And wise enough to know that my career probably had fifteen or twenty years at the most. Don't forget that I'd learned independence at my mother's knee. When I left home, I swore I would never delegate control of my life to another. During those years in Hollywood, I had a manager, a lawyer, an investment counselor, a voice coach, directors, producers. But in all those years, I answered to no one except myself."

"Not even a husband." The words seemed to escape B.J.'s lips before she could think. Out of the corner of her eye she could see Adam's hands tighten into fists. Without looking at him, she could sense his anger.

"Not even a husband." Nora stood and walked toward the doorway. Her voice was low, with no hint of pain or anger. "I'm afraid our family has a history of independence. And breaking all the rules." As she passed her son she touched his arm in a symbol of affection. "You seem to have decided to carry on that tradition, Adam."

The door closed softly.

"That was uncalled for."

"Yes. It was."

Adam studied her for long, silent moments. "What's eating you, Jess?"

She closed her notebook and strode to the floor-to-ceiling windows with their view of Central Park. With her back to him, she muttered, "A person is the sum total of everything that has occurred in the past. By discovering your mother's parents and early years, I expect to have better insight into the person she became." Her voice lowered, as if speaking to herself. "Yet here is a woman who, more than most, should have yearned for a husband and family."

"You're forgetting the fact that she was driven to become an actress. That sometimes means giving up a normal life."

"Her agent, Martin Stone, suggested that Nora's career just—happened. That she was a natural."

"And you believe that? Did her dancing career just happen? Or hasn't she told you yet about the hours she practiced the grueling routines, working until she dropped from exhaustion, so she'd be the best in the chorus line, and get the coveted spot center-front?"

B.J. turned to face him. "No. She didn't tell me that."

"And her financial success. Did she just happen to fall into that as well? Do you think my mother just started buying up land without any plan?" His voice mocked. "If you believe that, then you don't know Nora London at all."

She shook her head. "You're right, Adam. I don't." Her voice shook with conviction. "But I'm going to. Before I'm through, I'll know her better than I know myself." She gave a wry laugh. "Driven. An apt word. Beneath that sophisticated lady image lies a driven woman."

"What drives you, Jess?"

She turned away from his probing look and studied the teeming sidewalk far below.

"Truth. Knowledge. Facts. Getting inside someone. Giving the reader the best I can give. What drives you, Adam?"

With his hand on her shoulder, he turned her to face him. His eyes narrowed. His voice dropped to a low, seductive murmur. "At the moment, you. You're driving me crazy."

"Don't."

They had carefully avoided each other for days. The passion that simmered just below the surface needed to be denied if they were to continue to survive such close contact.

Adam never got tired of looking at B.J. Now, with the sunlight streaming through the windows, bathing her in its rays, she looked clean and fresh. He thought of all the wars in all those far-off places, with bombs and shellings, and screams piercing the blackness. If he had someone like this waiting for him, he'd never be able to go back to that hell. His career would be over. His freedom limited to her needs, her space.

B.J. felt him stiffen, and glanced up at his face.

He dropped his hand to his side. His tone was casual. "You've been cooped up in this place for days. When are you going to take time to see New York?"

"I'm here to work, Adam. And I wouldn't call spending my time surrounded by all this luxury being 'cooped up.'"

"Mother is having dinner with Martin tonight. Flynn's got tickets to the theater. It's a perfect night to do the town."

B.J. seized on one fact. "You mother spends a lot of time with Martin Stone, doesn't she?"

"Of course. They go back a long way."

"Have they ever been linked romantically?"

His voice hardened. "I believe that's her business, not mine. If you need to know, I suggest you ask her."

She turned away. "I will."

They both listened to the silence.

What was happening to him? Every time she got close, he forgot what she was doing here. She was here to open old wounds.

It was the thrill of the chase, he told himself. That's why his pulse raced and his palms grew sweaty each time they were together. He would have to have her. Soon. Living and working so closely together, it was inevitable. Then he'd be able to put it all in perspective. Then he'd be able to block her from his mind.

His hand touched her shoulder. His rough voice was laced with anger. "You haven't given me an answer."

"To what?" She felt the swift rush of heat at his touch.

In an exasperated tone, he said, "To having dinner with me." He thought about turning her to him and pulling her into his arms. He'd been thinking of little else for days.

She smiled. He could hear it in her voice. "All right. But can we keep it simple?"

He fought the desire to reach a fingertip to her cheek. "What do you think about a little wine and pasta in the Village?"

"That sounds simple enough. What time?"

"Seven." He glanced down at the cast on his arm. "It'll probably take me that long to get a shirt on over this thing."

"Then get started. I'd hate to go out in public with a half-dressed man."

"How about in private?"

She gave a short burst of laughter. "Don't try it, Adam. I've got two good arms to your one, remember?"

B.J. slathered on body lotion, then slipped on the white silk teddy, loving the feel of silk against her skin. She brushed her hair, leaving it to fall loosely over her shoulders, then frowned at her closet.

This was the first time she and Adam were actually going out together. She tried to dispel a tremble of fear. It was a dinner date. Nothing more. Yet she felt like an awkward teen on her first date. She had no right to encourage him. Hadn't she told him this could only lead to a dead end?

Mentally she shook herself. He was a big boy now. He could certainly take care of himself. And she'd been on her own now for too long to behave like this. They were going to dinner. That was all.

Adam had said simple, so simple it would be. Pulling on a winter white cowl neck sweater and white woolen slacks, she slid her feet into low white suede boots and grabbed up a fleecy white wool jacket.

She glanced in the mirror. Too wintry. From a drawer she retrieved a bright red mohair scarf and tied it about her throat just as a knock sounded on her door.

He had planned to say something clever. Instead, the words died in his throat. Her hair spilled down her back in lush waves. Her cheeks picked up the color of her scarf. Her dark eyes were wide, her lips curved in a smile of greeting. "I like a woman who can be ready on time. Come on." He caught her hand and led her along the hall to the elevator.

Adam was dressed in gray corduroys and a white fisherman's knit sweater. Over that he had pulled on a gray jacket, leaving one empty arm hanging limply. B.J. glanced at the threads dangling from the sweater sleeve that had been roughly pulled over the bulky cast.

"I see you managed without any help."

"And ruined a favorite sweater."

Instead of pushing the lobby button of the elevator, Adam punched the lower level, for the parking garage. As they stepped out into the bright lights of the underground garage, he led her to a sleek black Porsche.

"And I thought you were going to have me whistle for a cab." She gave the car a measured look. "Very nice, Mr. London."

Adam held the door while B.J. settled into the passenger seat. "I think anyone who'd drive in New York has to be a little crazy," she said as he turned on the ignition.

"It helps." He jammed the little car into reverse, backed around a Mercedes, and rolled from the sheltered quiet into the din of the streets.

With one hand, he smoothly threaded the car through traffic and turned onto a one-way street just ahead of a screeching taxi.

"Are you sure you weren't the driver of that Jeep that overturned in Central America?"

"Who said I wasn't?"

"That's a comfort." She grinned and leaned back in the glove-soft leather. Actually she enjoyed the speed of the little car. It was odd—with Adam driving, she felt safe. In fact, doing most things, she would feel safe with Adam. Most things. Her heart leaped at the thought of Adam's touch, then slowly returned to normal.

Amid the shops, galleries and restaurants that made up Greenwich Village, Adam smoothly guided the sports car into a narrow parking spot and caught her hand.

"There's a little Italian place just down the street that makes the best lasagna in the world."

"Good. I forgot to eat lunch today."

"And breakfast, from the looks of you." His gaze traveled over her slim figure before he wrapped his arm around her shoulders.

Inside the restaurant, as in all the places in the Village, the atmosphere was relaxed and casual.

The owner, barely five feet tall and at least as wide, wore a floral dress and white apron. Her dark hair was braided and twisted into a crown around her head. She greeted Adam like a long-lost son, raining kisses on his cheeks and chattering in broken English.

"Rosa, this is Jess," Adam said when he could get a word in.

"I give you the best table in the house," she said proudly, leading them to a table in front of the fireplace.

A carafe of red wine was placed on the table, along with two goblets. B.J. sipped the dry wine and smiled in contentment.

"This is exactly what I wanted."

His voice was low. "This wasn't all I wanted, but I'll settle for this, for now."

She felt a thread of danger at the tone of his voice, and dismissed it.

Adam watched as the warmth of the fire enveloped B.J., giving a rosy glow to her cheeks. Her eyes gleamed in the firelight. He felt the swift surge of desire. She was so lovely, he ached to touch her.

There were no menus. The food simply arrived, course after course of it, from salad with delicate oil and vinegar dressing, to thick, minestrone soup and hard-crusted rolls that melted in their mouths, to the entree, homemade lasagna.

"Did you grow up here in New York?" B.J. asked casually.

"Part of our time was spent here. My early years were spent in Paris, and most holidays in Switzerland. I didn't really feel like an American until my college days."

"Harvard, I believe."

He smiled easily. "For four years. And then U.C.L.A." The smile grew. "That was the real Americanization of Adam London."

"Where do you make your home now?"

"Nowhere. Anywhere. I'm as comfortable in New York as I am in Paris. But I especially love Gstaad. Mother has always kept a home in Switzerland. The people there are warm, friendly. They feel like family."

"Is family important to you?"

Adam studied her a moment, then gave her a lazy smile. "I think, Miss Conover, I've just been interviewed without realizing it."

She sipped her wine, avoiding his eyes. "Sorry. I didn't mean to do that." She looked up, meeting his gaze. "I can't help it. It's what I do." Just then the dessert cart arrived, diverting their attention.

For those daring enough, there was rich black coffee and canolis, the delicate pastries with a heavenly cream filling and topped with nuts and chocolate shavings.

"Want to try the dessert?" Adam reached a hand across the table to cover hers.

She stared at the hand, so strong, so large it completely hid hers. When she glanced up, his gaze was centered on her lips. She parted them slightly, and his grip tightened.

"Is it sinfully rich?" she asked the hovering waitress.

At her nod B.J. grinned. "You did say you're paying, didn't you?" She gave Adam a sly glance.

"Yep. My treat."

"Then I definitely want dessert."

Adam watched with admiration as she polished off two canolis and two cups of coffee.

"I don't understand where you put it."

She leaned closer. "Actually, I'm stuffing it in my bag. That way, I won't have to face Gerta in the morning. I'll just hide in my room and eat cold lasagna and gooey pastries for breakfast."

"I don't get it," he said with a straight face. "Gerta's always so cheerful. Why would you want to hide from her?"

"You're not the bearer of the poison pen. The only way I'd be less popular around that apartment is if I suddenly developed the plague."

Adam threw back his head in laughter. "We have been a little cool, haven't we?"

"Cool? You call that cool? I've seen frost form on the tablecloth when Gerta sets down my cup of coffee."

The warmth of his laughter washed over her. "Tell you what. From now on I'll knock on your door when I'm going downstairs for breakfast, and you can join me. Gerta wouldn't dare treat you badly in front of me."

"Yes, I've noticed that she's just a little partial to you. But, Adam London, if you dare knock on my door in the morning, I won't be responsible for what I do. I don't like to be disturbed when I'm sleeping. And when I am, I warn you, it's not a pretty sight."

He caught her hand. His thumb traced her palm, then moved to the pulse beat at her wrist. "I'll be the judge of that." He grinned at the look of surprise on her face. "I'd like to see you in the morning, Jess, still lost in sleep."

"I wake up alone."

"By choice?"

She avoided his eyes, not liking where this conversation was going.

The waitress arrived with their bill. Adam left the money on the table, then helped B.J. on with her jacket. At the door he slipped one arm into his jacket, then strained to catch the other lapel. Seeing his distress, B.J. turned and reached around his neck to draw the jacket over his cast.

"Want this buttoned?"

He stared down, amusement lighting his features. "No. It would never make it. But if you could just pull it together more."

"Like this?" With each hand gripping a lapel, she drew the jacket closed.

Adam's smile faded. It was replaced by a curious mixture of pleasure and pain. His arm came around her, pinning her firmly against him. "Mmm, Jess. You smell good. Feel good too."

His lips brushed hers lightly, with feather soft touches, until he felt her hands curl into his jacket, pulling him closer. Ignoring the swirl of snowflakes and the people passing by, he drew her against him and took the kiss deeper, feeling the instantaneous flare of heat.

"Jess." He spoke her name inside her mouth. She took in his warm breath and his words together. "You're becoming an obsession with me."

Disconcerted, B.J. made a move to push away. Adam held her firmly against him and covered her mouth. Desire seized her again and this time she didn't withdraw.

"Do you want me to stop?"

"No." She wondered if she had actually answered him, or imagined it. Her word was swallowed up by his kiss. She never wanted it to end. She was being swept along on a wave of such intense desire that it shattered all her notions of cool control.

"No. No." She plunged her hands deep into his hair and drew his head lower. Her pulse raced at an alarming rate. It was getting harder to breathe. The world had faded. She was warm, too warm in all these clothes.

Beneath her jacket, his hand stroked her sweater-clad back, then slid beneath it, to find the silk teddy.

"What's this?" He smiled in the darkness. "Silk next to your skin? Beneath all that maidenly white clothing beats the heart of a sensuous woman." While his fingertips stroked, his lips moved over her temple, murmuring her name. He brought his lips across her cheek, then down to the corner of her lips, then lower still, to the little hollow of her throat.

She arched her neck, loving the feel of his lips on her skin.

The delicate floral scent of her lotion mixed with the heat of their bodies. He was drowning in the scent of her. Catching a handful of her hair, he reveled in the silken texture. Drawing her head back, he rained kisses on her collarbone, her throat, before coming back to her mouth.

He had to have her. It was torture to hold her, to taste her, and not have all of her. A groan escaped his lips.

B.J.'s hands curled around his neck, drawing him closer. She'd never known such passion. The taste of him, the feel of his body against hers, was catching her up in a mindless world where nothing mattered except this man.

The restaurant door opened, and a laughing party of six raucous customers exited.

"Excuse me, buddy. Didn't mean to interrupt."

Amid loud laughter they stood on the sidewalk, whistling for a cab.

Adam brushed a stray strand of hair from B.J.'s cheek. Staring down into her face, he could see her lips still swollen from his kiss. Her cheeks were the color of her scarf; her eyes were rounded in surprise.

"Come on," he said almost gruffly, catching her hand.

His jacket blew open in the chill wind.

"Let's find someplace a little more private."

Chapter Five

With no wasted motion, Adam headed the Porsche toward the apartment. He touched a button on the dash and a singer softly crooned a moody love song. Beside him, B.J. still reeled from the effect of his kiss.

For a moment his hand left the wheel. He reached out to her in the darkness and his cool fingertips caressed her warm cheek. In the kaleidoscope of flickering streetlights, she closed her eyes, loving the gentle way he touched her.

Her eyes blinked open as he pulled his hand away. A moment later he dropped a gold lighter into her hand. It was warmed by his touch.

"Would you mind lighting my cigarette? I can't manage three things at the same time."

He shook a cigarette from the pack and set it between his lips. Steadying the wheel, he leaned toward her. A flash of light illuminated them as she held the flame toward him. His gaze burned over her as he inhaled. His eyes were molten silver, full of desire. A moment later a curl of smoke wafted toward the open window. She snapped shut the lighter, leaving them in darkness. She was trembling. Just sitting beside him had her nerves jangling. No man had ever affected her like this.

Adam drove with controlled urgency along the crowded streets. With an effort he swung onto the ramp and showed his identification to the parking attendant. Nodding his approval, he pressed the button raising the crossing bar and Adam gunned the car forward. Two rows down he found an empty space and parked the Porsche perfectly, with only inches to spare.

As he helped B.J. from the car he pulled her close against him. She could feel his impatience as he waited for the elevator.

"Cold?" He stared down at her upturned face and fought the desire to kiss her. If he did, they'd never make it upstairs.

"No." As she shook her head her hair tumbled about her face and shoulders.

He caught a handful of hair and watched through narrowed eyes as the strands sifted through his fingers. Bending toward her, his arm came around her waist, inexorably drawing her to him. She leaned toward him, anticipating the kiss. The elevator jolted to a stop, and a passenger stepped in. Stiffening, B.J. saw the glint of devilish laughter in Adam's eyes.

"She gets off at six," Adam whispered against her ear. "Then we'll have this to ourselves."

B.J. shivered and slid him a glance.

At the sixth floor the passenger exited, and Adam's hand tightened at her shoulder. "We're almost there."

It was the longest elevator ride of B.J.'s life. She stared straight ahead, counting the numbers as they flashed on and off. She had no doubt what Adam intended, and though she was terrified of the feelings his touch unleashed, she couldn't deny that she wanted him every bit as much as he wanted her.

When the elevator came to a stop at the top, Adam caught her hand. He opened the door, and with a smile that hinted of excitement and danger, led her inside.

"Home at last," he murmured against her temple. Draping an arm around her shoulders, he drew her close.

As they moved silently past the library, they both glanced up in surprise.

"Adam. Jessica. How lovely. Martin and I are enjoying a nightcap. Join us."

Like two conspirators, they paused awkwardly in the doorway. A fire crackled invitingly, the scent of cherry wood sweet in the air. Nora was reclining on the leather sofa, with a mohair afghan across her lap. She wore an elegant beaded sweater in softest blue that accented her eyes.

Martin stood at the bar, fixing drinks. He gave them a friendly smile. "Well, this is nice. You two out seeing the town?"

"The Village." Adam stood back to allow B.J. to enter first. "Thought we'd give Gerta the night off."

In the warmth of the room B.J. hesitated, then shed her jacket and scarf.

"What'll you have?" Martin asked. "Nora and I are having brandy."

"I'll have the same," B.J. said.

"Make it four." Adam strolled across the room and stared a moment at the flames in the fireplace. With his arm resting on the mantel, he studied his mother for long seconds, forcing himself not to look at B.J. Then, almost as if compelled, his gaze moved over her, seeing the slight flush of her cheeks, the way she avoided looking at him.

He wanted her more than he had ever wanted any woman in his life. At this moment he wanted to pick her up out of that damned chair and carry her off to his room. To hell with what the others thought. His hand clenched into a fist at his side.

Martin walked closer and handed Adam a
drink. With a grim smile, Adam tilted back his
head and drained half the liquid. Nora and B.J.
were making small talk. Martin handed each of
them a glass, then settled himself comfortably in
one of the big leather chairs. He lit a cigar and
puffed contentedly, then began regaling them with
stories from the glorious past.

Reminding himself that he had to be civilized,
Adam set his drink on the mantel and fumbled for
a cigarette. He reached in his breast pocket for the
lighter. It was missing. He glanced at B.J. and remembered that he had given it to her. With an ex-
aggeratedly careless stride he crossed to her.

"My lighter."

"Oh." She reached into her pocket and handed
it to him. As their fingers touched she felt a new
stab of desire, quick and urgent. She glanced up
at him with heat staining her cheeks, then quickly
averted her gaze.

Martin was in rare form. Within minutes he had
Nora once more reminiscing about her early days
in Hollywood. B.J., sitting stiffly across from her,
smiled in all the right places.

Too tense to relax, Adam walked back to the
fireplace and leaned a hip against the bookcase,
watching. God, he loved watching her. He had
enjoyed being with her tonight. She laughed easily. She was bright, interesting, without taking
herself too seriously. Yet she had managed to

glean a few facts from him without any effort. He resented that. He hadn't wanted to tell her about himself. It was something he never did, with anyone. Somehow, with Jess, it was easy to talk. That puzzled him. He had never opened up about his past before. Why now? Especially with this woman, who intended to expose his illegitimate birth to the whole world?

Her own past was another story. Despite her intelligence and humor, he knew nothing about her. She gave away very little about herself.

He sipped his brandy and studied her. Did she wear her hair in pigtails when she was a kid, or was it long and loose and wild? Had she been a tomboy, or one of those prissy little girls who hated bugs and dirt? He almost laughed. He knew the answer to that without asking. Beneath that proper facade he'd glimpsed a teasing scamp. Though she looked like an angel, the laughter of the devil lurked in her eyes. He sensed she was a woman who played by the rules, unless they got in her way.

"Remember, Adam?"

He turned toward his mother. "Sorry. I was drifting. What were you talking about?"

"The first week Flynn worked for me. That incident with the Hollywood gossip columnist?"

"Oh. Yes, I remember." Adam grinned. "Poor Flynn. She figured that marked the end of the shortest career in history."

B.J. was hooked. "What gossip columnist?"

"Aubrey Madden." Nora's voice nearly shook with emotion. "He was probably the most despised man in Hollywood."

Martin explained, "In his column, Aubrey had vowed to get an exclusive interview with Nora London. To that end he flew to New York one winter when Nora and Adam were in town briefly." He turned to Nora. "You came here specifically to hire a secretary, didn't you?"

Nora nodded, swirling the amber liquid in her glass. "Flynn came to me with excellent credentials and references. Because I had been fighting with the press for so long to retain my privacy, I just assumed anyone I hired would be aware of that fact. However," she said with a wry smile, "I forgot to stress that point with my newly hired secretary." She took a sip of brandy, then set the snifter on the coffee table.

"You were twelve, Adam. Do you remember?"

He nodded.

To B.J. she said, "I took Adam to the theater. A matinee. Afterward we had an early dinner. We probably returned here around six o'clock. Flynn looked all flushed and eager. A little flustered, I thought. As if she had some wonderful secret she was dying to share." Nora laughed and shook her head. "Some secret. Aubrey Madden had arrived at the door, fed her some concocted story about having an appointment with me that evening, and bluffed his way in. Poor Flynn bought every lying word of it. She showed him to the library"—she paused, lifting her hand to encompass their quarters—"this very room, and ordered Gerta to prepare coffee."

Adam glanced at B.J. She was sitting on the edge of her chair, staring intently at his mother.

That was it. That was her talent. That was how people opened up to her. She had that rare ability to listen, really listen, to what they were saying. In those wide, green eyes lurked interest, absolute fascination, with what was being said. The drink on the table beside her was forgotten now. Even, he thought with a pang of regret, the promise of passion that had flamed between them. Her entire being was now centered on the story unfolding from his mother's lips.

Nora's eyes glittered at the memory. "Flynn was so proud of her efficiency. She met us at the door to tell me the good news. Imagine. Aubrey Madden, the most infamous columnist of the day, in our very apartment." The actress laughed once more at the memory. "Flynn was beaming, expecting me to be pleased with her. She nearly died when she saw my expression turn from pleasure to horror."

Adam nodded. "Mother's face was as dark as a thundercloud. She grabbed my hand, turned on her heel, and hissed in that haughty tone that was her trademark, 'We shall return in one hour. If that— *monster* is still here, I'll have your head. If he won't go, phone the police. Then see that this apartment is swept clean of all vermin. If you must, phone for an exterminator.' With that, she hauled me off to the Museum of Modern Art, where I got a fascinating hour-long lecture on contemporary artists.''

"Did Aubrey Madden give up?'' B.J. asked.

"Not that man.'' Nora gave a sound of disgust. "In his next column he bragged about spending over an hour in Nora London's luxurious apartment, 'filled with mementos of her beloved days in Hollywood.' He went on to describe everything he could remember, and a number of things he invented, just to fill up space. He never admitted being ejected, but simply said that after a day at the theater and dinner, Nora London and her young son were too tired to say more than a simple hello to all his readers.''

"He did the same to practically every star,'' Martin interjected. "If he couldn't get an interview, he simply made one up. After some of the things he reported, more and more stars began refusing him interviews. Remember what he did to Stephen Hart?''

Adam walked to the bar and poured another drink. They were never going to be able to slip away now. Martin was loosening his tie. Nora was warming to the subject. He sighed, and tried not to think about the fascinating creature whose warm and pliant body had set him on fire just a short time ago.

He flexed his stiff shoulders. His arm was starting to itch again. He longed to tear off his cast and scratch the burning skin. He forced himself to ignore it.

His gaze wandered to B.J. She was an itch. No, an ache, and one that couldn't be ignored. Each time they came together, he left feeling raw and wounded. It was far more painful than the injuries he'd sustained in the accident. Those were healing. But this—there was no cure for it. He had to have her. Thoughts of her were getting in the way of his work, his sleep.

Adam crossed the room and sank down in the chair next to B.J.'s. Stretching out his long legs, he sipped his drink and forced his attention back to Martin. This had definitely not gone the way he'd planned it. It was going to be a long night.

"Tell Jessica about Aubrey's run-in with Stephen Hart," Martin urged.

Nora nodded. B.J. tucked her feet under her, wishing she had a notebook. Her drink was forgotten now. She would need a clear head to remember all these details when she got to her room. She wanted to record every detail tonight before going to sleep.

"I think it was Stephen's third wife." The actress paused, then nodded. "Yes. Yvette, the beautiful French actress he had met while filming

A French Affair. I didn't get to know her very well. Their marriage lasted only a little over a year." Nora chuckled as she added, "It was short, but memorable. Yvette, hoping some publicity would boost her developing American career, invited Aubrey to their house for an interview. Unfortunately, she forgot to tell Stephen." She glanced up at B.J. "I believe I once told you that Stephen was very charming. He was also notorious for falling in and out of love constantly. At the time of this interview he was filming a new movie called *Mexican Melody*."

B.J. nodded excitedly. "I've seen it on the late show at least a dozen times. I still love it."

Nora smiled. "It is a lovely film, isn't it? Do you recall the fiery Mexican dancer, billed only as Montez?"

"Yes. She danced on the table top, then fell into his arms."

"That's the one," Martin said dryly.

"The day Yvette had the interview with Aubrey was the same day Stephen, on a wild impulse, brought Montez home. Midway through the interview, the two of them strolled out of the bedroom, looking a bit too rumpled to have been simply practicing their dance routine."

B.J. leaned forward. "What happened?"

"Have you ever seen a cat fight?" Martin asked with a rumble of laughter.

"In front of Aubrey Madden?"

"Umm. And through his pen, in front of the entire world. His column was probably picked up for syndication by a dozen more newspapers because of his description of that little scene."

"Did it hurt Stephen Hart's career?"

"Are you kidding?" scoffed Martin. "That sort of thing only made him the hottest property in Hollywood."

A thread of anger colored Nora's tone. "But it reaffirmed the double standard. Although Stephen's career seemed to grow with every scandal, both Yvette and Montez were never considered for a serious role again. They were reduced to bit parts."

"And Aubrey Madden?" B.J. asked.

"Although many of the stars despised him, they were forced to cooperate with him. The studios courted favor with him, knowing his stamp of approval could guarantee a film's success." Nora's voice trembled with fervor. "He was privy to a great many secrets. If he was crossed, he showed no mercy. He wielded his power like an evil dictator."

B.J. had to ask the logical question. She forced herself not to glance at Adam. "If you hated him so, why did you grant him an exclusive interview twenty years ago?"

"I didn't." Nora took a long moment to sip her brandy. As she placed the glass back on the table, it sloshed over the edge and continued to drip along the side, forming a wet ring. Quickly, Nora dropped her linen napkin beneath the glass. She glanced at Martin before turning to meet B.J.'s look. "It was another of his inventions. He made up the entire interview. When I left Hollywood, I left it for good. Since I was no longer making movies, he had no club to hold over me. I didn't need Aubrey Madden. I didn't need the studio. And I certainly didn't care what the gossips whispered behind my back."

Nora London was a gifted actress. She could play any role convincingly. B.J. would have believed her, except for one thing. For one unguarded moment, there had been a trace of something—fear perhaps—in her eyes. Blinking, B.J. studied her carefully. Whatever it was, it was gone now. She took a sip of brandy and puzzled over it, allowing the conversation between the others to slip by her unnoticed.

Aubrey Madden. B.J. remembered coming across his name in her research. She had even read the interview. It touched on several intimate subjects, including Adam's academic life and his love of photography. Could the gossip columnist have invented such a thorough picture of Nora and Adam London's personal life? She made a mental note to dig deeper into this. There was something here she had overlooked.

"I have tickets to the theater Friday night, Martin," Nora said, breaking into B.J.'s thoughts. "Would you like to join me?"

"Sorry. I'm flying to the coast." Martin began straightening his tie. He stood. "And I'd better get home. I have an early flight." He shook Adam's hand, and B.J.'s, then bent to kiss Nora's cheek. "Don't get up. I'll see myself out. I'll call you next week."

When he left, Nora removed the afghan and stood. With a smile at her son, she caught B.J.'s hand and strolled toward the door with her.

"I'm glad you two joined us. I don't often enjoy reminiscing, but how can I refuse with such an attentive audience?"

Walking along the hallway, she continued to lean on B.J.'s arm, then turned at the door to her suite. "Good night, Jessica." She leaned toward Adam and kissed him lightly on the cheek. "I must admit, I've enjoyed having you here, darling. I believe this is the longest we've been together in years." Her voice lowered. "I've missed that." Nora paused for a moment, then brightened. "I'm so happy to see you mending so well, but the truth is, I'm going to hate to hear the doctor say you're well enough to go back."

"Then don't think about it. It's going to be a few more weeks before I'll hear those words." He held her close in a hug. "In the meantime, Mother, let's enjoy our time together."

With a weary wave of her hand, she closed the door.

"Your mother seemed worn out, Adam. Are you concerned?"

He glanced at her as they climbed the stairs toward their rooms. "She does seem to tire more easily these days. But the truth is, I haven't been around her enough lately to make a judgment. I suppose it's just her age."

B.J. shrugged. "Adam, why wouldn't she tell me the truth about that interview with Aubrey Madden?"

He paused. "What do you mean?"

"I did my research, Adam. The interview is on record for anyone who cares to read it."

His voice had the harsh edge of anger. "If you want an answer, ask my mother. I have no intention of giving you material for your book, Jess."

B.J. struggled with her thoughts. Why couldn't she shake off this vague sense of doom?

When they reached her door, Adam made a move to open it. B.J. stopped him. "I'm going in alone, Adam."

He gave her a lazy smile. "I thought I'd join you."

"No."

"That isn't what you said a while ago."

She licked her lips. "I've had time to—cool off."

"Umm." He smiled down into her eyes. "Then I'll warm you." His arm came around her, pinning her against him.

She felt the heat, swift, urgent. It was going to take all of her willpower to resist him.

As he dipped his head she turned. His kiss caught her on the cheek.

"No, Adam."

"Why?" His voice lowered, with a hint of anger.

"I think we were about to make a terrible mistake. We were fortunate this time. Your mother and Martin got in the way."

"Don't try to deny what you felt, Jess."

She swallowed. "I'm not."

"This kind of magic doesn't happen between every man and woman."

"No."

His voice lowered to a growl. "Then why not just accept the fact and enjoy it?"

"Adam," she said, trying for patience. "I'm not denying the feelings I have. But I learned a long time ago that I can't have everything I want. Some things just aren't good for me." Her voice deepened with emotion. "And you're one of them."

He lifted a hand to her cheek. Rubbing his knuckles across her skin, he watched the flame leap into her eyes. "I'd never hurt you, Jess." He bent his lips to hers. As if burned, she drew away.

"Not intentionally. But we'd hurt each other, Adam. We're bound to."

He caught a loose strand of her hair and tucked it behind her ear. Tracing her earlobe with his fingertip, he studied her. "There's no stopping it, Jess. We're going to be living under the same roof for too long to fight it. Sooner or later, we're going to come together."

"Maybe." She evaded his look. "But we both know where we're headed. In a few weeks you're going back to your dirty little war. And when I'm through here, the things I'll be forced to reveal will cause you anguish."

He nodded solemnly. "Don't you think I've faced that?" His voice was nearly a whisper. "If I could turn and walk away from all this right now, I would. But we're stuck here together, Jess. And before it ends, we're going to have to come to terms with it."

As she started to speak he added, "It's all right, Jess. I've got all the patience in the world. When you're ready, I'll know."

She turned and opened the door. "Good night, Adam. Thanks for dinner. Next time, I'll buy."

The angry tone of his voice surprised her. "Damn right you will. I'm starving, and you're the only one who can feed this hunger."

"Oh Adam…"

He caught her arm. His voice, so near her ear, caused her to jump. "Just don't lie to yourself,

Jess. You told me you believed in facts and truth. The truth is, there's something between us that won't let us rest until it's satisfied.''

B.J. pulled away and began to close the door. His words were hardly more than a whisper.

"There's no stopping it, Jess. There'll be other nights."

She closed the door firmly, trying to shut out his words. What she needed was hard work. Tough mental stimulation. It had always been her cure for an attack of restlessness. She hurried to her dresser, grabbed up a notebook and began writing furiously, jotting down all the things Nora and Martin had said. Names, she thought, trying to pull all that she'd heard from her brain. How many names had they mentioned this night? Nibbling on her lower lip, she concentrated, blocking out all thought of Adam. She wouldn't think of him. She wouldn't. This book was her ticket to the top. She couldn't let her feelings for him get in the way.

An hour later she stood and flexed her cramped muscles. She stripped off her clothes and pulled on a pale, silk gown, which molded itself to her slim contours. Drained, she walked to the windows for a last glimpse of the city at night. As her hands grasped the drapery pull, she saw a wisp of smoke curl about the balcony outside.

Adam.

All she needed to do was open the door to the balcony. The ache deep inside her would be assuaged. For tonight at least, he would fill her arms, and her needs.

But what about tomorrow, and all the tomorrows she would have to face, while she picked apart his mother's life and opened all those secret wounds?

Shivering against the cold, she closed the draperies and turned out the lights. In the lace-bedecked bed that had reminded her of a princess's bed from her childhood stories, she lay awake, listening to the words of warning echoing in her mind.

She wasn't royalty, and this wasn't pretend. In real life, people didn't always live happily ever after.

She rolled to her side and tried to block out the image that sprang unbidden to her mind. A knight, dark, angry, forbidding. Adam, with his rogue's smile, offering her passion, danger, excitement. But only for the moment, until he rode off once more in search of other, more worthy opponents.

She fell asleep listening to the sounds of the city and her wildly beating heart.

Chapter Six

It was holiday time. The city of New York groaned under the weight of a second major snowfall. Whenever she could, B.J. walked the snow-covered paths of Central Park. The acrid scent of roasted chestnuts from vendors' carts drifted on the frosty air. Frenzied shoppers filled the streets, along with harried workers. The din of traffic, sirens, horns, whistles, shouts mingled with the merry sound of bells rung by Santas on every street corner.

By completely immersing herself in her work, B.J. managed to hold Adam at a distance. Although they shared the same work space, she often closed herself in her room when she heard the sound of Adam's typewriter. It was painful to be so near him. When they had to work in the same room, she was scrupulously polite. But sometimes, when she was typing, B.J. was aware of Adam watching her from across the room. It was as if he were waiting for some signal from her to approach.

Nora London seemed to miss an unusually large number of her afternoon appointments. Whenever she was informed by Flynn that the reclusive actress was unable to see her, B.J. found herself again wondering if Nora was regretting her decision to bare her past.

It was a gloomy day, with snow falling on and off since early morning. B.J. alternately typed and flipped through her notes. Nora's childhood had already been thoroughly discussed in their talks. She had provided albums and assorted photos, along with letters and diaries. The actress was amazing. She had kept records of every aspect of her life. Almost as if, B.J. thought, she had known that one day she would want them as reference material.

The door to her workroom opened. She glanced up to see Flynn.

"Miss London won't be able to meet with you today."

Inwardly B.J. groaned, while outwardly she remained composed. "I'm sorry. Is she ill?"

"No," Flynn said quickly. "Some conflicting appointments. We'll try tomorrow."

"Thanks, Flynn." B.J. watched her walk stiffly away, then reluctantly returned to her typing.

A short time later the door opened. Without glancing up, B.J. called, "Have our plans been changed again?"

"You might say that."

At the familiar sound of Adam's voice, she turned. He stood in the doorway, a silly grin splitting his face. For long moments she simply stared. Then it dawned on her.

"Your cast. Oh, Adam. How wonderful. They've removed your cast."

He strode across the room. His smile was dazzling.

"How does it feel? Good as new?" She stared at his arm. It seemed strange to see him without the ungainly cast. If possible, he seemed even taller, stronger, more self-assured.

He slipped off his jacket and flexed his arm. "So damned weak. I can't believe how much strength I've lost."

"Good. Want to arm wrestle?"

"You would take advantage of my weakness, wouldn't you?"

"I warned you. Any advantage I can." She grinned. In a more serious tone, she asked, "Did the doctor recommend therapy?"

"Yes." He frowned. "Just another excuse to keep me from my work."

She struggled to keep her tone even. "You really can't wait to get back to your war, can you?"

He studied her for long, silent moments. "So it's *my* war now, is it? What do you think?"

She didn't have to think; she knew. He'd been away too long—she could sense his restlessness. She turned away from him. "Now you can catch up on your work. Typing ought to be good therapy."

"I can think of more entertaining ways to exercise." His voice lowered as he slipped his arms around her waist.

B.J. recoiled as if burned. "So can I."

"Damn it, Jess. You keep avoiding me."

She backed up. With her hands on her hips, she said, "All right. Here I am. What did you want?"

For long moments he studied her while she faced him defiantly. She was barefoot, dressed in jeans and a pale pink sweater, her hair held away from her face with tortoiseshell combs. It spilled wildly down her back in a cascade of curls.

"You know what I want." He took the step that separated them and dropped his hands to her shoulders.

"But I don't know what I want, Adam."

His hands made slow, hypnotic circles on her shoulders and upper arms. He watched the color rise to her cheeks.

"I think you do."

He drew her closer and saw the flames leap in her eyes. "This is the first time I've been able to hold you in so long," he murmured against her temple. "Oh, Jess, you feel so damn good."

Summoning all her willpower, B.J. pushed herself from his arms. When she was free of his embrace, she tossed him a wadded-up piece of paper.

As he caught it she warned, "I told you to stick to your typing, Adam." Then she turned away and ducked into her bedroom, calling, "Those are the notes you couldn't finish typing yesterday, because your arm was bothering you so much. Remember? You dropped them all over the floor. You can start with them."

"You're a barrel of laughs, Jess. But you can't keep running forever."

She poked her head around the door before she slammed it shut. "And when you finish those, just look on the floor. There are plenty more where those came from."

For the rest of the week Nora failed to keep her appointments with B.J. Each day, Flynn appeared at the door with her regrets and no further explanation. On Friday, B.J. looked up from her typing to see Flynn approaching.

"Miss London will see you today." At B.J.'s sudden smile of relief, Flynn added, "Since she's a little under the weather, she'd like you to come to her bedroom."

"I'll get my notebook."

B.J. was ushered into the cheerful bedroom on the lower level of the apartment. It was her first visit to this intimate room.

"Jessica." In a mound of pillows, Nora reclined in a king-sized bed. Snowy linens edged with handmade lace formed a pristine backdrop for the pale figure in an ivory satin bedjacket. "I'm so sorry to have slowed things down like this. I'm afraid I've picked up a virus of some sort."

"It can't be helped. I hope you're feeling up to this." As she moved closer B.J. noted the pallor beneath the artfully applied makeup. "If you'd like to wait a few more days..."

"No." The actress lifted a hand to stop any further protest. "I'd really like to talk today, if you don't mind working in here."

B.J. glanced around the cozy room. If this room reflected its owner, then Nora London was a homebody at heart. It had the artless elegance of a French country cottage. The walls and thick carpet were white, but everywhere were brilliant splashes of color, from the hand-crocheted bedspread of wildflowers, to the colorful settee done in a petit point of lush roses. Two matching upholstered chairs were covered in pale rose chintz. A round table beside the bed held dozens of framed photographs of family and friends. An antique writing table along one wall was filled with more framed pictures.

A fire crackled in the fireplace, the scent of wood-smoke blending with the delicate fragrance of lotions and soaps from the adjoining bathroom.

"Do you mind if I look at the photographs?" B.J. asked.

"Not at all. I'll explain them as you look," Nora offered.

There were dozens of pictures of Adam, from chubby-cheeked toddler to student to bearded adult.

"That was Adam's fourth birthday. He's wearing the sweater my friend Carolyn knit. Wasn't he a darling?"

B.J. couldn't help smiling at the innocent in the photo. Beside him stood his mother, helping him blow out the candles on his cake. To the other side of him stood a smiling blond woman, clutching the arm of a bemused, dark-bearded man.

"These are the Thompsons?" B.J. held up the photo. She had seen photos of the man before, but not his wife.

"Josh Thompson, the director, and his wife, Carolyn, who was my dearest friend."

B.J.'s gaze skimmed the photos. Here was Adam, a young teen, waving from the platform of a train. There was Adam, on skis, standing beside a clean-shaven Josh Thompson at the top of a mountain slope. Picking up a very old photo, B.J. studied Nora, at nineteen or twenty, and a young, beautiful Carolyn, in practice tights, standing at the barre.

"It was our love of dancing that first brought us together," Nora explained, seeing the picture in B.J.'s hand. "When I first arrived in Hollywood, I joined a dance class to stay limber. I met Carolyn, and we introduced ourselves by our first names only. A few weeks later I confided to her how nervous I was because I was auditioning for Mad Thompson. Everyone had warned me he was a tyrant. Carolyn only laughed and told me I'd be wonderful. Then, seeing how nervous I really was, she offered to come along to give me courage. All through the audition she sat quietly in the corner, smiling, nodding encouragement." Nora laughed, remembering. "After the audition, I caught her hand and dragged her toward the director, intending to introduce them. Imagine my shock when Mad Thompson took her in his arms and embraced her."

B.J. turned to stare in amazement at the actress.

Nora laughed. "My reaction exactly. Then they explained that they were husband and wife. But because Josh was already so successful, Carolyn often didn't mention their relationship to strangers. That way, she knew if people liked her for herself or in the hopes of currying favor with her husband.''

"Did you get the part?"

Nora smiled. "Yes. And the lifelong friendship of two wonderful people."

B.J. continued to study the photographs. "Who took all these pictures?"

"Josh took many of the early ones. As a director, he had a good eye and enjoyed photography." Her voice warmed. "Many of the later pictures were taken by Adam. Josh gave him his first camera when he was only six. From then on he was never without it."

"With all that influence, did you ever think Adam would go into filmmaking?"

Nora looked down and smoothed the sheets. "Hollywood was never Adam's town. He would have evoked only curiosity there. I saw to it that he was a citizen of the world."

B.J. set down the picture she was holding and moved toward the bed. "You didn't like Hollywood much, did you?"

"Oh, yes. Not at first, of course. I was a New Yorker, and my heart was always here. But I learned to love it. It broke my heart to leave. Yet I knew that beneath the glamour was another, darker side. I didn't want Adam to have to see that part of it."

"How could it be avoided?"

"By cutting it out of my life completely. For all its worldwide appeal, Hollywood is a small town. Everyone knows everyone else's secrets."

B.J. swallowed and forced herself to speak. "And Nora London had secrets she didn't want whispered about."

Nora surprised her by smiling gently. "My scandal rocked not only Hollywood but the world. And it has dogged my footsteps ever since."

"You were at the peak of your career when you had Adam. The most acclaimed actress in Hollywood. How could you bear to turn your back on all you had achieved?"

Nora's voice softened. "My work was all I had. By then, my mother had died. All around me were families, sharing so much more than just success." She stared pointedly at B.J. "How old are you, Jessica?"

"Twenty-eight."

"It will happen sooner than you think. One day, I woke up and realized I was thirty-three years old. I had wealth and fame. And my life was empty." She smiled gently. "Today's woman would say my biological clock was ticking. I only knew that I wanted more out of life than what I had."

Her words echoed through B.J.'s mind, touching a familiar chord.

As B.J. opened her notebook Nora closed her eyes for long moments. When she opened them, she saw the look of concern on B.J.'s face.

"I'm fine, really, Jessica. Just a little tired. Now, what shall we talk about today?"

B.J. gave her a gentle smile. "Let's continue on a topic that seems to make you very happy."

At Nora's quizzical look she added, "The Thompsons. There's a light in your eyes when you speak of them. Tell me more about them."

Nora snuggled deeper into the cushions. "Carolyn was my first friend in Hollywood, and remained my friend through everything. Our love of dance was a common bond in the beginning. But it was more than that. We liked the same things, disliked the same things. Someone could be talking, and we needed only a glance to know what the other was thinking. She could make me laugh with just a look or a word."

"And her husband?"

"Josh adored her. They were the happiest, most loving couple I've ever known." Nora's voice warmed to her topic. "When we first met, Josh was so proud of her talent. She was the best natural dancer I've ever seen. I had to push myself to the limit to beat the others. But not Carolyn. There's no doubt she would have gone on to become the most celebrated dancer in movie history."

"Why didn't she?"

Nora's fingers fussed over the lace edging on the sheet. "One day in class she fell. Not during a difficult routine, but just a simple dance step. She wasn't hurt, just surprised. A few days later it happened again. This time she was badly bruised. When it happened again while we were walking to lunch, I suggested she see a doctor."

During a pause, B.J. listened to the ticking of an antique clock on the mantel.

"It was nearly a month before she saw a specialist. He told her that she was showing signs of the early stages of a gradually debilitating disease. He warned her that she would soon be walking with a cane."

"Was there nothing she could do?"

Nora shook her head sadly. "Nothing. Although she tried for a few more months, she eventually had to give up her beloved dancing completely."

At B.J.'s shocked look Nora said, "Josh went into a state of depression. He phoned specialists everywhere, took her to the finest clinics in the world. In the end, they were both forced to accept her fate."

"How soon did she need a cane?"

"Before she was thirty." Nora pointed to the picture of the smiling adults around Adam and his birthday cake. "Take a closer look at that."

Nora picked it up and brought it close to the bed. "Why?"

"See how heavily Carolyn is leaning on Josh's arm? Her cane was left out of the picture. In fact, we always moved the cane before snapping photos of her."

As B.J. returned the photograph to the table, Nora said, "By the time Carolyn was forty, she was in a wheelchair. And for the last fifteen years of her life, she was confined to her bed."

"How did her husband accept her disability?"

Nora watched B.J.'s pen fly across the notebook. "He was devoted to her. He spent his entire life making her happy. They were the most loving couple I've ever known."

B.J. glanced up. "No children?"

"No."

"Did her illness leave her unable to bear children?"

Nora's finger traced the lacy outline of her sheet. "Carolyn didn't want to bring a child into the world if she couldn't care for it. Even though at first Josh couldn't accept the doctor's verdict, I think Carolyn sensed how difficult it was going to be for her. Josh was a bit of a dreamer, an eccentric. She was always the levelheaded one. So when he talked about a family, Carolyn gently demurred."

"Do you think she ever regretted her decision?"

Nora shook her head and smiled. "They had Adam. They lavished him with love and attention. They never missed a birthday or Christmas. No matter what Josh's shooting schedule was, they managed to be with us on all the important days. And he returned their love. Adam always accepted them as part of our family." Her eyes glowed. "Carolyn loved Switzerland as much as I. She and Josh spent his last days there with me."

"He died two years ago, I believe," B.J. murmured, still scribbling.

"Yes. And Carolyn died there last year. I was with her to the end. We spent so many wonderful holidays in Gstaad. Those are still my happiest memories."

Closing her notebook, B.J. stood. The actress glanced up in surprise.

In an unusually gentle tone B.J. said, "Then on that happy note, I'll leave you to rest."

"But we've barely talked this week. You must be growing impatient with me, Jessica."

"I have more than enough work to keep me busy." She saw the relief on Nora's face. What had it cost her to keep her appointment today? "If you're feeling up to it tomorrow, we'll talk some more." She took the pale hand in hers. "Rest now."

At the knock on the door both women turned. Adam stood a moment, his gaze fixed on their joined hands, then crossed the room to his mother's bed.

"Gerta wonders if you're feeling up to dinner tonight."

"Tell her I'll just have some soup and hot tea in my room. For now, I intend to sleep."

B.J. moved toward the door. Adam bent to brush his lips over his mother's brow before walking from the room.

In the hall his tone turned to ice. "Have you said something to upset her?"

"Don't be ridiculous. Why would I want to upset such a lovely person?"

His frustration was evident in his sarcastic tone. "You mean you haven't found anything sordid in her past yet?"

"I'm not looking for anything ugly. I'm here to record your mother's life. If it's been a beautiful life, that's even better." Her voice lowered. "Adam, believe me, I'm not trying to pass judgment on your mother."

He passed a hand over his eyes. "I know. It's just that she looks so damned frail."

"Yes. She said she's had a virus. Has she seen a doctor?"

"Flynn saw to it. Still, I'm worried."

"Maybe you'd feel better if you spoke to her doctor."

He nodded. "I think I will." As she turned to walk away he dropped a hand to her arm, stopping her. "Have dinner with me tonight, Jess."

"I don't think—"

"I do." His deep voice, so near her ear, sent shivers down her spine. "You've been ducking out every chance you get. Stay here tonight."

She hesitated. "Will Gerta dump hot soup in my lap?"

"You know better than that."

"Yes. I was only teasing." She turned to stare into his gray eyes.

They crinkled as he laughed. "You'll stay?"

"Why not? Gerta makes much better food than the deli."

Adam stood by the tall windows of the living room, staring out at the lights of the city. His vague sense of dissatisfaction was growing. It wasn't like his mother to stay this long in New York. She preferred the quiet life in Gstaad, or their lovely cottage outside Paris. Since she'd been here, she and Flynn went out nearly every day. And when she wasn't out, she was resting. It was so out of character for her.

Why had she commissioned this book? She had spent a lifetime jealously guarding their privacy. Now she spent hours telling Jess stories about her career, and even her private life.

And this virus. She had never been sick a day in her life. Now, for the first time that he could remember, she seemed frail, vulnerable. He didn't like it. But his attempts to talk to her about all of this were gently rebuffed.

And Flynn. She seemed to be evading him. He rubbed his stiff arm. After all these years with Nora London, Flynn was a master of secrecy. She gave away nothing.

He turned at the sound of footsteps. B.J. was wearing black silk evening pants and a pale pink silk blouse that emphasized her slenderness. She had piled her hair on top of her head and secured it with jeweled combs, leaving the ivory column of her throat exposed above the deep V neckline, bare of adornment. Adam thought about the taste of her skin, and fought the urge to take her in his arms.

"Drink?"

She nodded. "Whatever you're having."

He stood at the bar and poured Scotch over ice. B.J. watched, remembering how awkward it had been for him the last time. Now he seemed comfortable, in his element.

She moved to the wall of windows. "Did you speak to your mother's doctor?"

He handed her a glass and stood beside her. "I tried. He was out. I left word for him to phone me."

They stood without touching, staring out at the lights of the city.

"Is Flynn joining us?"

"No. There's just you and me."

She detected a thread of danger in his tone, and ignored it. They'd been alone before. She could handle it.

"Your mother talked about the Thompsons today. Josh and Carolyn." Walking to the sofa, she sat down, settling herself comfortably into the corner. "They meant a great deal to her."

"Yes." He watched her a moment, then crossed the room and sat beside her. He caught a trace of her delicate cologne. Obviously she had given up trying all the perfumes and lotions in the guest room. He preferred hers. "Carolyn became the sister she never had."

"It must have been good for you as well. Your mother probably wanted you to have a few strong men in your life."

He chuckled. "Proper male rôle models, right?"

She flushed.

"It's all right, Jess. I'm not sensitive." He leaned back, relaxed and sipped his drink. "Would you like to hear about the men in my mother's life?"

She shot him a quick glance. Was he teasing her, or did he actually intend to volunteer some information?

"There was Martin Stone, of course. You've met him. What do you think?"

"I like him. He seems to thoroughly enjoy your mother's company."

Adam nodded. "He'd better. He's been a part of her life for over fifty years."

"Do you like him?"

"How could I help it? Martin has always been the elder statesman of the family. He's kind, caring, dependable. He was the one we always called on in an emergency. He has good common sense. He's solid, shrewd in business, tough and overly generous where my mother is concerned. I've always thought of him as an uncle."

B.J.'s mind began calculating. Could Martin and Nora have been lovers all these years?"

"And there was Klaus, Gerta's husband."

B.J. glanced up.

"He was the hardest-working man I've ever known. A quiet man who always got things done. He was fiercely political." His tone grew thoughtful. "It was Klaus who never let me forget how important freedom is to the human spirit."

His thoughts were interrupted by Gerta.

"Dinner is ready, Adam."

He glanced up with a smile. "Thanks, Gerta."

Taking B.J.'s hand, he helped her up and escorted her to the dining room. At his simple touch she felt lightheaded. It had been weeks, and still she could recall the fire of his kiss.

Beside Adam's chair was an ice bucket. Gerta uncorked the bottle. "Here's the wine you selected," she said quietly before returning to the kitchen.

Adam poured two glasses of pale amber wine and handed one to B.J. She sipped.

"Umm. Nice."

"So are you, Jess." He stared into her wide, dark eyes; as always, she looked incredibly desirable to him.

Silently, Gerta brought in two salads and a basket of rolls, fresh from the oven.

B.J. broke a roll and watched the butter melt. Taking a bite, she laughed. "Definitely better than the deli." Seeing Adam's relaxed smile, she said, "Tell me about Stephen Hart. Did you get to know him well?"

Adam chuckled. "He practically boarded with us between wives."

"Why?"

Adam thought a moment. "I guess he couldn't bear to be alone. He was always surrounded by a lot of people. And when the others got too busy to pamper him, he turned to us. We were like his family, I suppose."

"Did you like him?"

Adam's eyes danced with laughter. "Like is too mild a word. You'd have to know Stephen. He was completely undisciplined. He was undependable, shallow, vain, a terrible prankster." He shook his head at the memory. "Yet he was funny, utterly charming when he wanted to be. He was silly. A big tease. I always thought of him as a brother. In the early years, like a big brother. But as I grew older he seemed more like a kid brother."

"You make him sound like a paradox."

"Definitely. He inspired very strong feelings in people. You loved or hated Stephen Hart. There was no middle ground." Adam's voice softened. "I loved him. Mother did too."

All the old rumors she had read rushed through B.J.'s mind. It could have been true then. Stephen Hart could have been Adam's father.

As Gerta cleared away the salad plates and lifted the covers on two silver plates of Dover sole garnished with small potatoes and fresh vegetables, Adam caught B.J.'s hand.

"You're transparent, Jess. Stop trying to figure the answer to the puzzle."

She felt a blush stain her cheeks. Pretending interest in her dinner, she pulled her hand away and began to eat.

Adam poured more wine. Over the rim of his glass he said, "I suppose Josh Thompson was the single biggest influence in my life."

"Everything I've read about him indicates a gifted, moody, tyrannical director, who drove stars to temper tantrums with his imperious ways."

Adam laughed. "That's pretty accurate."

"Were you afraid of him?"

Adam stared at her in surprise. "Afraid of Josh? You must be joking."

"But..."

"He was all those things people wrote about him. He was brilliant, intense, demanding as much of himself as those around him. He was driven to be the best." Adam's gaze strayed to the crystal chandelier over the table. The mark of a fine craftsman was evident in the work. "He bought this in Ireland. When it arrived, I watched him examine every one of the prisms, to be certain none of them had been damaged during shipment. This was a special gift to my mother, and he wanted it to be perfect." He smiled at B.J. "That's the kind of perfectionist he was. I used to watch him at parties. He was uncomfortable in large gatherings. But alone, just the two of us, I felt all his energy focused on me. No matter how busy his schedule, he always had time for me. He was a kind, nurturing person. When he bought me my first camera, he took me out in the village and showed me how to frame a shot, how to see, really see, through the eyes of the camera. He had just finished filming a movie that would eventually win him an Academy Award. He was exhausted. Yet he took time to show me the intricacies of photography." Adam's voice grew warm with the memories. "That's the kind of man Josh Thompson was. When I was a little kid, I used to wish he was my father."

"And now?"

He glanced at B.J. His expression hardened. "It doesn't matter anymore."

"Don't deny it, Adam. It has to still matter. It will always matter. You have a right to know. Haven't you ever asked Nora?"

He smiled at her anger. Covering her hand, he said, "It was an unspoken command. When I was younger, and asked, she became hurt, withdrawn."

"And now?"

"I never mention it. I can't stand to hurt her any more." He lifted her hand, measuring its small softness against his own strength.

"But it's going to appear in print, Adam. The whole world is going to know."

His gaze moved up to her face. "I know why I'm upset, but why are you so angry, Jess?"

Why? She didn't know. It was as if—the thought stunned her—she was sharing his pain. It was ridiculous. She was here to do a job, not to become involved. Yet she ached for him.

"Because it isn't fair. You have a right to know who your father was."

"I will." He studied her in the light of the chandelier. "Who said life is fair?"

Pulling her hand away, she stood abruptly. "Stop being so damned understanding about it. I'm writing a book about your mother's life, Adam. And it's your life too."

His voice was a low rasp of restrained fury. "Don't you think I know that? Have you forgotten how hard I fought this?" He paused for long moments, staring at her rigid back. The tick of a grandfather clock in the foyer could be heard in the silence. His voice softened. "I've had to learn to live with infamy. I've become a master at putting a good face on it."

Gerta entered and began clearing away the dishes. A minute later she carried in a silver tray with coffee and dessert.

Adam smiled at her. "Thanks, Gerta. Dinner was lovely. I'll take this in the living room."

The old woman's gaze lingered on his face a moment, giving him a warm smile. The smile faded as she glanced at B.J., still standing awkwardly by her chair.

Picking up the tray, Adam led the way to the living room. He set the tray on the coffee table, then poured a cup for B.J.

She prowled restlessly around the room, stopping to touch an unusual figurine, then moving to study the signature of a lovely painting. Adam stood by the windows watching her. She was clearly agitated. As if, he thought with sudden clarity, she was suffering his agony.

"Jess."

She stopped.

"Coffee or wine?"

"I've had enough wine. I can't think."

He lifted a plate of hand-dipped chocolate cherries. "There's no need to think. Come and enjoy the dessert Gerta made."

She laughed suddenly. "I see that you know my weakness."

His voice lowered as she walked closer. "I'm making a list of them to use to my advantage."

"Then I'd better have some coffee to clear my head."

Sinking down on the sofa, she picked up a confection and savored the rich chocolate and cherry. "Umm. Heaven."

"You can afford a few more." Adam's gaze trailed her slender figure, then came to rest on her mouth as she devoured a second candy. He sat down beside her, with his arm resting along the back of the couch.

She felt the first tiny threads of excitement begin to unravel her composure. The coffee and sweets lay forgotten on the tray. He was going to kiss her. Although he didn't move, she could almost feel the pressure of his lips on hers.

Adam stared down into her face, knowing what she was thinking. She was anticipating his every move. She was the unpredictable one, always throwing him offguard with her erratic moods. It was time she had a taste of it. Though her lips were just inches from his, warm and inviting, he resisted.

He leaned closer. "I like your hair up."

Her eyes widened a fraction.

"It makes your throat so accessible."

He ran a fingertip along her jaw to her neck. Hypnotized, she moved against his finger. Without warning, his lips followed, brushing open-mouthed along the creamy column of her throat.

B.J. put a hand to his chest to steady herself. Deep inside her something tightened. Tiny ripples of pleasure coursed through her veins.

Seeing her stunned expression, Adam lowered his mouth again, brushing his lips along the other side of her throat, then dipping low to the little hollow between her breasts.

Her hand curled into his shirt and he caught it, holding it tightly while his mouth continued brushing soft kisses against her skin.

The ripples became giant waves of sensations sweeping her along in the tide. Drugged, she lifted her face to him.

He studied her lips, parted in invitation. Warm, drowsy from the wine, she waited to welcome his kiss. She had missed the danger, the excitement of Adam's touch. She longed for it.

Seeing her heavy-lidded look, the way her lips invited him, Adam nevertheless fought the desire that raged through him. He would make her want him the way he wanted her. Thoughts of her had tormented him, robbing him of sleep, getting in the way of his concentration. Now she would feel the same need.

Releasing her hand, he reached up and removed the combs from her hair. It tumbled in waves about her face and shoulders. He felt a tightening in his stomach. He wanted to thrust his hands into the tangles and revel in the lush softness. Cupping her face, he touched his lips to her eyelids, then traced the curve of her cheek, before moving to her ear. Still, he didn't kiss her lips.

Breathless, waiting for his kiss, she moaned in impatience. Passion became a raw hunger, leaving her weak and limp.

Adam fought the passion that pulsed, denying the need to draw her to him, to feel the softness of her body. His hands plundered her hair as his lips nuzzled her ear. Without realizing it, he breathed her name as his lips whispered over her skin. Taking her lobe between his teeth, he nipped, and heard her little moan of pleasure. He tried not to get lost in the delicate scent of her cologne. With unbelievable tenderness, he kissed her temple, her forehead, her eyelids, until he heard her moan again.

She wanted to pull him to her, but she lacked the strength. Drugged, her eyes closed as he continued to press soft kisses against her face, she lay against the pillows of the sofa, feeling his breath warm on her skin.

"Adam, please." Her voice was low, throaty.

"Please what?"

"Hold me."

"I can't."

Her eyes fluttered open. "You have two good arms now."

"But I can't hold you, Jess." His voice sounded as husky as hers. He fought the almost overwhelming desire to crush her against him.

Adam's excitement flared anew as he realized his power. With a little persuasion, he could have her. He could finally end this terrible tension between them. But that wasn't what he wanted now. What was happening to him? He wanted it all. Her mind. Her body. He wanted her warm and willing, and as hungry as he was. He wanted to know her past as she knew his, what she loved, what fears gnawed at her, what drove her to push herself so fiercely. He wanted her to open to him.

Her breath came in short little gasps. Her heartbeat was erratic. Her eyes were dark with desire.

"When?" She was amazed at how difficult it was to speak.

"When you know what you want, Jess."

"Adam."

He brought his face closer. His lips hovered above hers. It took all his willpower to keep from kissing her, from taking her now.

"When you decide, let me know, Jess."

He was courting her, he realized. Such an odd, old-fashioned word. It sounded like something from his mother's era. It didn't apply to either of them. Courtship? That was a prelude to commitment. Marriage. Something he couldn't consider in his line of work. He couldn't take a wife to war. What did he want then? Right now he wanted Jess. What held him back? Caution? Or fear? Whatever it was, it sapped all his strength. On legs that threatened to fail him, he walked from the room, leaving her alone and empty.

Chapter Seven

Can you be packed this afternoon?"

B.J. stared at Flynn for several seconds. She had stayed in her room, trying to ignore the tantalizing aroma of coffee wafting from the kitchen, until she was certain Adam had finished breakfast. She told herself she wasn't avoiding him. She just needed to be left alone. Without her caffeine, her brain refused to function.

"Packed. I don't understand. Why would I pack?"

"Miss London has decided to spend the holidays in Gstaad."

"Oh." B.J. felt a small stab of pain. She had hoped to spend the holidays working. That way she could pretend they didn't exist. For her, holidays were always a painful reminder of those earlier times, when her mother would decorate, bake, shop, and then wait by the phone in the hopes that her father would come home to join them. Until that phone call, B.J. never knew whether it would be a joyful celebration or a day of depression. She remembered those bleak holidays after her father's death. The days had seemed interminable. The nights were spent listening to her mother's muffled weeping.

"Do you think she's well enough to make the trip?"

"Apparently she thinks so." Flynn waited in the doorway of B.J.'s room.

Gnawing on her lower lip, B.J. shook her head. "This is a personal time. Nora and Adam deserve to spend their holiday alone, without my intrusion. I have enough work to keep me busy here. Tell Miss London that I've decided to go back to my apartment until you return."

Flynn nodded.

Listlessly, B.J. began gathering her supplies. She closed the portable typewriter, then began sorting through her notes. By the time Nora and her entourage returned to New York, she would probably have the manuscript up to date.

She paused at another knock on her door.

"Miss London insists you join us. She thinks it will improve her biography if you observe first-hand her life in Switzerland."

It made sense. Still, B.J. was reluctant to intrude. "I don't think—"

"Once her mind's made up, Miss London won't accept any argument. We leave for the airport at three."

B.J. stared at Flynn's retreating back. Three o'clock. No time to think. What in the world did she need? She raced to her closet and began rummaging through her clothes.

Downstairs, at precisely three o'clock, two limousines waited at the curb. Nora, Gerta, Adam and B.J. were helped into the first. Flynn traveled in the second with the luggage.

At the bustling terminal B.J. watched in awe as Flynn took charge. A dozen assorted pieces of luggage were counted and tagged. The secretary handled their tickets, while Nora and Gerta were placed in an electric cart and delivered effortlessly to the gate.

"Did you know about this?" B.J. asked Adam as they threaded their way along the endless walkway.

"Are you kidding?" He took her elbow as a crowd passed them. "The last I knew, Mother could barely crawl out of bed. This morning she's determined to leave."

"Is this typical, Adam?"

He smiled. She noticed the way his tired features relaxed. "Yes, I'm afraid it is. I grew up never knowing where I'd spend tomorrow." He gave her a sideways glance. "I like it. It keeps me on my toes."

It explained why he had seemed so restless in New York. It also explained why he was willing to cover all those wars in all those countries. He still never knew where he'd spend tomorrow. She gritted her teeth. He liked it that way.

The 747 left on schedule and they were soon airborne. B.J. marveled at Nora's stamina. Though she ate lightly, she talked and read until nearly midnight before she turned off her overhead light.

B.J., uncomfortably aware of Adam beside her, fought the feeling of disorientation until exhaustion overcame her. Then she was vaguely aware of Adam tucking a blanket around her. She thought she dreamed that he lifted her head gently and placed a pillow beneath. It seemed to her that his hands lingered in her hair for long moments. Then all was forgotten. High in the air, she slept.

A hand brushed the hair at her temple. A soft, whispering sound signaled the shade being lifted at the round window of the plane. Soft light bathed her in its glow. Her lids fluttered, then opened. Adam's face was close to her, watching the brilliant sunrise on the horizon.

"I didn't mean to wake you. I just wanted to watch you in the light of the morning." His warm breath feathered her skin, causing tiny tremors along her spine.

"What time is it?"

"Dawn. Look at the greeting London is giving us."

She turned her head to study the ribbons of scarlet trailing the winter sky.

Adam had studied her, so open, unguarded, in sleep. Now, awake, he watched as she struggled to compose her features. He was shocked at the rush of feelings as she touched his arm.

"Oh. It's so beautiful. How much longer?"

"A couple of hours here at Gatwick. We'll go through customs here. We should be at Berne around noon."

After their inspection at customs they breakfasted at the international airport, where they switched to a much smaller plane for the flight to Berne, Switzerland.

During the two-hour flight to the Swiss capital, B.J. pressed her face to the small window of the plane, watching the flat terrain gradually change to majestic mountains.

"This is what I'd hoped Switzerland would look like. But Adam, it doesn't seem real. It looks like a painting."

He chuckled. "It's almost too beautiful, isn't it?"

She nodded, pleased that he understood what she meant. They sat in companionable silence, enjoying the breathtaking view of snow-capped mountains and tiny, isolated villages.

At the airport, as they were helped into waiting limousines, Adam murmured to B.J., "I think you'll enjoy this part of the trip, Jess. Mother always gets a special car on the Swiss Federal Railroad."

B.J. glanced at Nora. Swathed in sleek sable, from the flowing coat that reached to the tops of her boots, to the matching hat that she wore jauntily to one side of her silvery hair, she looked every inch the movie star. Though her face was still pale and her features drawn, there seemed to be more spring in her step as she walked to the Montreux-Oberland railway that would take them the final sixty miles to their destination.

Inside the elegantly appointed railroad car, Nora settled herself into a plush reclining chair. Flynn dropped a mohair throw over her lap, and Gerta proceeded to prepare a snack from the contents of a huge hamper. Before the train started they were sipping champagne and nibbling caviar and wonderful Swiss cheese and biscuits.

Adam watched B.J.'s face as she stared out the window at the throngs of people. Voices clamored in French, German, Italian and English. When the train began moving, she watched as the ancient streets and arcades of the capital city, termed the Federal City by its residents, flowed past her line of vision. Everywhere there were lovely fountains, and old buildings with oriel windows and towers. They passed sandstone steps worn smooth by generations of Swiss passing this way over the centuries.

Once out the city B.J. stared openmouthed at a snow-covered countryside with forests, hills, glaciers and small mountain lakes, sparkling like diamonds in the brilliant sunshine.

An hour later the train slowed.

"We're here." Adam's voice, so near B.J.'s ear, caused her heart to lodge in her throat.

The little village of Gstaad nestled in the Saane Valley. At the railway station a sled, pulled by a team of horses, stood ready.

"Otto." Nora beamed as the bearded driver removed his cap and bowed slightly.

Offering his hand to the actress, he helped her into the sled and covered her lap with a fur throw, then assisted the others.

"Otto, this is Miss Conover."

"A pleasure, Miss." He tipped his hat and handed Adam a fur, which he immediately dropped over B.J.'s lap.

"Otto's been meeting our train for years. And before him, his father was our driver," Adam whispered to B.J. "Look at Mother's face now, Jess."

She turned to glance at the actress. Nora's eyes danced with excitement. Her lips curved in a smile of contentment. Her skin glowed in the frosty air.

Otto and another man loaded the mounds of luggage into a wagon, which would follow their sled. While fresh snow continued to fall, muting the horses' hoofbeats, they glided through the colorful village, past the bright shops and ginger-bread houses with sloped roofs. Bells tinkled in the frozen silence as they passed a herd of cows. Straining up a steep incline, they came to rest before an elegant chalet.

While the men wrestled with the suitcases, the women hurried inside. B.J. paused in the middle of the open great room and stared around with an expression of awe.

Massive timbers formed the exposed beams of the ceiling. The walls and floors were wood, gleaming with the patina of age. Brightly colored rugs were scattered throughout the rooms, adding warmth as well as pattern. An open, four-sided fireplace dominated the room. Around it were sectional sofas of pristine white. Colorful afghans stitched with patterns of flowers and birds were draped artlessly about the furniture.

While the others bustled about, B.J. roamed the room, noting the hand-painted ceramics, the signed paintings, all adding warmth and love to the room.

She picked up a delicate vase and studied the initials.

"Carolyn's."

She turned at the sound of Adam's voice. "All of these?" She indicated the vases, animals, flowers, all done in ceramics.

"Yes. After she was confined to a wheelchair, she needed an outlet for her energy and creativity."

"The paintings as well?"

Adam nodded.

Her gaze swept the lovely room. "Seeing this place, I think I know her better. No wonder your mother loved her so much. Her vitality, her love of life are evident in her work."

"If Josh had the genius, Carolyn had the vision." Adam smiled as he studied the vase in B.J.'s hands. "While he taught me to see the truth through my camera, she taught me to appreciate the beauty."

"You were lucky to have known them."

With his knuckles, he traced the curve of her cheek. His voice lowered to a murmur. "I want to know you too, Jess. Really know you."

She felt Adam's sensual pull and stepped back a pace, to break the spell. Still his gaze held her.

"Jessica." Nora paused in the doorway, surprised and pleased at what she saw in their faces.

B.J. glanced away, alarmed at what Nora's probing stare would uncover.

The actress smiled. "I'll show you to your room." As B.J. followed her the actress explained, "Actually, this house is two houses. This is the main house, with great room, kitchen, dining room, and suites of rooms for myself, Flynn, and Gerta. Gerta now occupies the room that was once Adam's. The guest house is separated by an indoor pool and sauna. It was originally built for Josh and Carolyn. It has its own kitchen, sitting room and adjoining bedrooms, separated by a large bathroom. The second bedroom was for Carolyn's personal maid, who bathed her, dressed her, and prepared her for the day and night." She smiled brightly. "The master bedroom is now Adam's. I think you'll be very comfortable in the adjoining bedroom."

While Nora spoke, B.J. stared openly around the beautifully appointed rooms. Although luxurious beyond belief, they retained a cozy comfort usually reflected in much simpler lifestyles.

It wasn't until they skirted the enclosed pool and entered the guest house that B.J. realized that she and Adam would be sharing very intimate quarters. The two luxurious bedrooms shared an enormous bathroom, complete with sunken tub and separate dressing areas.

Nora left her at the door of her room, and once inside, B.J. noted that her suitcases had already been unpacked. Her clothes hung neatly in the closet. Her toilet articles had been arranged in a large, mirrored vanity.

After kicking off her shoes, she sprawled across the bed and stared at the high, beamed ceiling. This was all too much to absorb. Christmas in the Alps. Sleigh bells, snow that looked whiter than anything she had ever seen in New York, and jagged walls of mountains. And Adam in the room next to hers. Overcome, she slept.

"Sleepyhead."

B.J. pulled herself back from the dark tunnel of sleep. With a supreme effort she managed to pry one eye open. Disoriented, she stared around the unfamiliar room, then remembered where she was. She was instantly awake.

Adam stood in the doorway. "I have to go to the *lebensmittel.*"

At her blank stare, he explained, "The grocery store. Want a tour of the village?"

"I'd love it. Give me five minutes."

After running a brush through her hair, she slipped into warm boots and pulled a down jacket over her jeans and sweater. Adam was waiting in the hallway.

Catching her hand, he led her down a slick incline toward the wide main road that traversed the town.

"Your home here is wonderful, Adam."

He smiled down at her. "Coming here always feels like coming home. There's a sense of family here. As often as we could, we spent our holidays here."

"It must be very important to your mother. This trip took quite an effort."

He nodded. "I was worried about her. But seeing how happy it makes her, I've decided it was the right decision. She's resting how. By tomorrow she should be much stronger."

They passed a bakery, and B.J. stopped. "Umm. What's that wonderful smell?"

He stared through the window. "Sugar cookies. Want one?"

"Yes. No. Make it two."

He grinned and bought a bag of lightly browned wafers sprinkled with colored sugar crystals. They were still warm from the oven. Before they emerged from the store, B.J. dug her hands into the bag and began munching.

"Oh, Adam. Look. A toy store."

They pressed their noses to the window, staring at the assortment of wagons, puppets and dolls. B.J. caught her breath.

"Ooh. It's the one."

"What?"

She pointed. "That antique doll. I saw one like that when I was a little girl." She laughed, a gay, tinkling sound in the crisp air. "I fell in love with her. I told my father she was the only thing I wanted that year for Christmas.''

"And you loved her and lived happily ever after until she fell apart."

At the sudden silence he glanced down at her. She looked away. "My father didn't make it home that year. Come on, let's find your lebens...grocery store."

She pulled on his arm, eager to move on. Popping a cookie into his mouth, he allowed himself to be led away.

At the store Adam produced a list Gerta had given him. As they piled the items on the counter, B.J. asked, "What in the world is all this for?"

"Gerta goes into a frenzy of cooking and baking for the holidays. I just do as she tells me, and manage to stay out of her way until she's finished. It's some sort of female ritual I've never understood. But I have to admit," he muttered, reaching for a bottle of exotic flavoring, "I always enjoy the fruits of her labors."

"I wonder if she'd let me help her."

As he paid the grocer in Swiss francs, Adam seemed surprised. "You cook?"

She held the door as he hefted the mesh shopping bag. "Badly. But I'm not a complete idiot in the kitchen." At his narrowed look she laughed. "I can scramble eggs. I don't burn the coffee. And once a year I like to try my hand at baking something special."

As they climbed the hill toward home, he shrugged. "You can ask her. Personally, I like to keep my distance from Gerta when she's busy. I've always been afraid she'd press me into service rolling dough or something."

She squared her shoulders. "I'm going to volunteer."

Adam opened the front door.

"Fine," he said, handing her the bag filled with groceries. "But if she attacks you with a rolling pin, don't say you weren't warned."

He hurried away, and B.J. carried the sack to the long wooden table. Gerta turned.

"I hope we got everything you wanted."

The old woman nodded as she began unloading jars and bottles.

B.J. cleared her throat. "I wondered if you could use some help."

Pale blue eyes studied her. "What can you do?"

B.J. thought about Adam's words. "I could roll some dough. Crack nuts. Measure ingredients. Anything you need."

With her hands on her ample hips, the older woman watched her a moment longer. Then she turned. "All right. You can start by rolling out that chilled dough and cutting out shapes with those cookie cutters."

With a happy smile, B.J. rolled up her sleeves and set to work.

"You'll need an army to eat all this," she said later, setting cookies on a baking sheet and popping one into her mouth.

Gerta rapped her knuckles with a wooden spoon. "Don't eat the dough. Wait until it has baked." She sighed at B.J.'s impish grin. "My niece has three little ones. They can eat three dozen."

"You have family here?"

Gerta nodded. "My brother's girl." She stared out the window a moment. "He was the first to get away."

B.J.'s head came up. Her reporter's mind sensed something deeper here. "Get away?"

Gerta looked at her. Dusting her hands on her apron, she said softly, "From our homeland. East Germany. Kurt took his wife across the Alps. A month later my husband Klaus and I followed."

"Weren't you frightened?"

The old woman looked away, but not before B.J. saw the look in her eyes.

"I was terrified. They unleashed the dogs. We could hear them baying. When they got too close, Klaus made me go on alone. Otherwise, he said, we'd both be caught."

"How did he get away?" The cookies were forgotten. B.J. moved toward the old woman.

"He didn't. In order to save me he offered himself up."

B.J. covered her mouth. In nearly a whisper she asked, "What happened to him?"

"He went to prison. Through some family members, I heard the news." Her eyes misted. "I would have lost faith, if it hadn't been for Miss London."

"What did she have to do with it?"

"When I came here, I needed a job. An official in the town sent me here. And when Miss London heard my story, she vowed to do everything she could to reunite me with my Klaus."

"How did she manage it?"

The old woman shook her head. "I've never known. She phoned everyone she ever knew who could have some influence. It took five years, but she managed it. One Christmas Eve, when we arrived at Gstaad, my Klaus was here waiting for me."

Tears streamed down Gerta's cheeks. "From that time on, Christmas Eve has always been special to me. Klaus was everything to me. My life; my love. He worshiped the ground Nora London walked on."

B.J. swallowed back her tears. "Were there no children, Gerta?"

The woman's head shook. "But we had Adam. How Klaus loved him. He spent so much time with him when Adam was a boy. He wanted him to appreciate the freedom he took for granted. My Klaus. And Nora London gave him back to me.

Because of her, we had the chance to spend the rest of his life together. No one will ever know how wonderful that woman is." Her voice was choked with sobs. "Can you blame me for wanting to protect her—even from you?"

Awkwardly, B.J. touched the old woman's shoulder. Her voice trembled. "No. No. Oh, Gerta, I'm grateful that you told me."

The cook lifted her apron and wiped away her tears, then turned back to the stove. Her voice threatened to break. "Why are we wasting time like this? I have some hungry people to feed. My adopted family. And tomorrow I'll be with my other family; my niece and her little ones."

Placing a tray of cookies in the oven, B.J. mulled over the things she was learning about Nora London. Saint or sinner, it no longer mattered. Like everyone who was touched by her, B.J. was beginning to care deeply about the aging actress. She hoped she would find nothing to change her mind.

Christmas Eve dawned clear and bright in the Swiss Alps. B.J. and Adam sat in the cheerful breakfast nook, sipping coffee. Morning sunlight descended from blazing mountain peaks, turning their snowcaps brilliant shades of red, purple, umber. The sun slowly flooded the valley below, bathing everything in its radiance.

"I see Gerta didn't throw you out of her kitchen."

She smiled. "My good friend Gerta? Why would she do such a thing?"

He shook his head, chuckling. "Good friends, hmmm? What's your secret, Jess?"

She ducked her head. "I just worked hard and listened."

Listened. He sipped his coffee and watched her over the rim of his cup. It was what she did so well. But she never talked about herself.

"What are you planning today?"

"I thought I'd work. I have a lot of typing to catch up on."

"Work? It's Christmas Eve."

Adam noticed the look that came to her eyes. Pain. Swift, fleeting. Then it was gone.

"I still have to do my work."

"Not today." He caught her by the wrist. "What's the matter, Jess? Didn't Christmas ever live up to your expectations?"

Her eyes widened.

"Come on."

"Where are we going?"

"Mountain climbing."

"Forget it."

"You do want a tree for Christmas, don't you?"

She eyed him suspiciously. "What's the catch?"

"Here in the Alps, we cut our own."

She twirled away. "Give me a minute to get my jacket."

Adam stood back and watched as B.J. placed the last ornament on the tree. Taller than Adam by a foot, it gave off a woodsy fragrance as it shimmered and glowed under the mantle of lights and colored balls.

She stepped aside. "It's beautiful."

"I think it's the best one we've ever had."

She sighed as she plugged in the lights. "I've never cut a Christmas tree before. It's special."

"Every Christmas should be special, Jess."

She bent and picked up the papers and cardboard boxes. Hugging them to her chest, she turned away.

Wrapped in a velvet dressing gown, Nora walked through the doorway.

"Oh, my dears. What a lovely tree."

"We cut it on the slopes."

"Did you tell Jessica what we've planned for tonight, Adam?"

"No, Mother. I'll leave that to you." Adam leaned a hip against the fireplace and lit a cigarette.

"Gerta is cooking a goose. We'll have a sumptuous feast. No company. This is a night for family." Her smile dazzled. "And that includes Flynn and Gerta and you, Jessica."

B.J. fought to keep her features from betraying the emotion she felt.

"There's a lovely monastery up in the hills. The monks have one of the finest choirs I've ever heard. On Christmas Eve we always go to their service at midnight. It's like being in the company of angels. You'll join us, won't you, Jessica?"

A knot of uncertainty started in the pit of her stomach. She was feeling out of her element. Swallowing back her fear, B.J. smiled. "I'd love to."

Nora waved a delicate hand. "Wonderful. I'll see both of you in an hour at dinner." She glanced at B.J. "I hope you brought something elegant."

B.J. grinned. "I hadn't even thought of it. But I'll manage."

The dress was silk, in an iridescent opal shade, with draped neckline and long, tapered sleeves. B.J. brushed her hair long and loose, then pulled one side back with a jeweled comb. Opals dangled from her ears. As she walked the dress picked up and reflected the glittering lights from the candles glowing about the room.

Adam added a log to the fire, then stood. From his position in the shadows, he watched her. She had a walk that drove him crazy. His gaze swept her, seeing the mass of waves that cascaded over one shoulder, the luminous quality of her eyes. She was so lovely she took his breath away.

The table was set for five with fine lace and crystal, china and silver. Gerta carried the goose on a silver platter. The table groaned under the weight of the international fare that Gerta had prepared with love.

Flynn floated down the stairs in an emerald silk dress with matching velvet jacket. Behind her, Nora descended, wearing a dress of palest pink antique lace, with a matching coat of pink cashmere.

"Ladies, you look lovely." The figure beside Adam stepped from the shadows.

Nora let out a little squeal of delight. "Martin. Oh, I can't believe it. How wonderful. How did you manage this?"

He kissed her cheek. "When I heard you had left for Gstaad, I decided to follow. I couldn't take another holiday in California. And New York would be empty without you, love."

Her eyes glowed. "Thank you, my dear friend." She glanced up. "Gerta. Set another place at the table. This is going to be a wonderful holiday."

B.J. couldn't recall an evening more special than this. Over champagne and oysters, goose and molded salads accompanied by freshly baked rolls, they talked and laughed while the flickering flames of the fireplace cast a warm glow over the room and its occupants. When at last they nibbled marzipan and drank strong rich coffee, the talk had turned to reminiscences of happy memories of years past.

Martin glanced at the diamonds at Nora's throat. "Josh gave you those in…" He thought a moment. "…forty-six, wasn't it?"

"Forty-seven," Nora said softly. "When we finished filming *The Pirate*. It had been an interminable ordeal. So many things went wrong, it's a wonder we ever finished it at all. Stephen's new bride used to show up on the set to glare at me during our love scenes." She glanced up at Martin and laughed. "How many times did you have to come over to smooth things out?"

"Dozens." He chuckled softly. "You burst into tears so many times we finally persuaded Josh to order a closed set."

She nodded. "Carolyn was considering giving in to her exhaustion and accepting a wheelchair. That was eating away at Josh. And I was so restless. My life was so unsatisfying…" Her voice trailed off.

The others around the table had gone very quiet.

Beside her, Adam reached for B.J.'s hand and squeezed it very tightly. At his glance B.J. averted her eyes. She couldn't bear to let him see what she was thinking. 1947 was the year Nora London left Hollywood in disgrace.

Martin broke the awkward silence. He scraped back his chair and walked around the table to embrace the actress. "Diamonds were the perfect gift for you, love. Warm, brilliant, priceless. The strongest stone on earth. Nothing can break them." He caught her chin and smiled down into her eyes. "Or you. Come on." He turned to include the others. "Let's get to that monastery and listen to the angels."

Chapter Eight

The night air was so crisp, so needle-sharp, it hurt to breathe. Sleigh bells announced the horse-drawn sled gliding effortlessly over the frozen landscape. Everywhere was a hushed expectancy. Snuggled beneath a fur robe alongside Adam, B.J. trembled. This night was magic.

To lift Nora's spirits, Martin began humming a familiar holiday refrain. Before long they all joined in. Their cheery voices, straining at the high notes, echoed in the night sky.

A church spire loomed in the darkness. Drawing nearer, they could see people streaming toward the lone building. Many walked or skied.

Some drove. A few chose the traditional horse-drawn sleigh.

The monastery was a towering structure of yellowed limestone cut from the surrounding mountains. Stained-glass windows glowed from the lights of hundreds of candles. Fragrant evergreen boughs, tied together with red satin ribbon, surrounded the massive wooden door pulls.

Adam and Martin assisted the women from the sled. Inside, the air was heavy with the sweet odor of incense. As their party seated themselves in a rear pew, black-robed monks paraded up the center aisle, each carrying a lighted taper, chanting words unintelligible to B.J.

When the choir was assembled in the nave of the church, the pipe organ began the first notes of a hymn. The classical music rolled and thundered through the building, reverberating around the domed ceilings. Adam caught B.J.'s hand and turned to her with a warm smile. Despite the heat from the crush of hundreds of people, B.J. shivered. Feeling the tremor, Adam caught her hand in both of his.

"Cold?"

"No. It's just this." She nodded to include the ancient pews, worn smooth through the centuries, the altar, a solid slab of gleaming marble, the flickering chandeliers that glowed with hundreds of white candles. "It's awe-inspiring." She didn't add that sharing all this with Adam caused her to tremble.

Fascinated by the pomp of the midnight cere-
mony, B.J. finally relaxed, allowing herself to get
caught up in the festive atmosphere. Maybe this
was what she lacked in her own life. Customs,
rituals. A sense of continuity. Since her father's
death, she had tried to ignore the annual celebra-
tions that reminded her of earlier disappoint-
ments.

B.J. glanced at Nora. With rapt attention she
was lost in the beauty of the music. Her gaze was
fixed on the life-size figures in the mural that
covered the ceiling. For too long she had had to
carry the burden of being a figure that to many
was larger than life. But in reality, B.J. realized,
Nora London was flesh and blood; a woman who
loved, and laughed, and cried.

Too soon the service ended. Streams of people
followed the monks down the aisle and out into
the frosty air. Voiced raised in French, German,
Italian, English, called out greetings.

The sleigh sped through the darkness and deposited them once more at their chalet.

"Gerta, we'll have coffee and brandy around
the fireplace while we open our gifts," Nora
called, swirling dramatically through the doorway in her fur.

"I'll help." B.J. hurriedly handed her coat to
Adam and followed the maid to the kitchen.

Sharing a conspiratorial smile, the two women
opened a cupboard door and began placing foil-
wrapped packages on a silver tray. While Gerta

prepared the coffee and brandy, B.J. added jaunty yarn bows to her gifts. When everything was ready, they emerged from the kitchen.

"What's this?" Adam poked at a small package on B.J.'s tray.

"Don't touch. It's a surprise."

"You didn't have time to shop."

"That's right. But I did have time to bake."

Nora's head came up. "You baked us something, Jessica?"

B.J. nodded. "While I was helping Gerta." She laughed. "I wanted to make something personal. This was the best I could do. They're gingerbread cookies."

She handed Nora the first one. Carefully unwrapping it, Nora smiled. "A star."

Silver sugar sprinkles had been added to the frosting to make it sparkle.

"Appropriate," Martin chuckled.

"And yours, Flynn," B.J. said.

The secretary tore the foil from her package. The cookie was square and flat. With frosting, B.J. had added white lines and a squiggle of yellow frosting that resembled a pencil.

"Not a very good notebook," B.J. mumbled.

"It's perfect. I think I'll hang it on the tree instead of eating it." Flynn turned and flashed the first warm smile she had ever offered her. "Thank you, Jessica."

B.J. walked to the maid. "Yours, Gerta."

The old woman seemed touched and surprised that she had been included. When she tore off the foil wrapping, she saw a cookie shaped like a rolling pin. Everyone laughed.

"I'm afraid I didn't know you were coming, Martin. But since I baked a few extras, this one reminded me of you."

He unwrapped a jolly Santa cookie.

"If you don't mind, I'll eat mine," he said, laughing, and he bit off the head. He rolled his eyes heavenward. "It's wonderful. You're a good cook, Jessica. If you ever decide to give up writing, you can always come bake for me."

"But you'd soon grow tired of gingerbread." She laughed and handed the last package to Adam. "This one's yours," she said almost shyly.

His eyes met and held hers a moment before he unwrapped it. It was a gingerbread man whose arm had been broken off, then replaced with frosting in the shape of a sling.

"You won't believe this. I originally intended to put a camera in his hand, but his arm broke by accident. That was when I got the idea for the sling."

He laughed as he passed it around for the others to admire. "I'm going to follow Flynn's lead and hang it on the tree. This is too special to eat just yet."

He nestled it in the branches of the tree, then touched his lips to B.J.'s cheek. "Thank you."

She felt the little curls of pleasure along her spine.

The others began exchanging packages. Flynn received a cashmere robe from Nora. Adam placed a flat package on his mother's lap. With a puzzled look, she opened it. Inside were dozens of enlarged photographs.

She gave him a dazzling smile. "Oh, Adam. All those old faded photographs. You've made them better than new."

"I knew how much you treasured them," he murmured, bending to kiss her.

"Jessica," Nora called. "This is for you."

B.J. was surprised and touched that the actress would think of her at such a special time. Accepting the small package, she opened it to find a pocket-sized tape recorder.

"Your fingers are forever flying across the paper while I speak. I thought this would save you some time."

"Thank you. I'm not very good with gadgets. But I'm sure with a little practice I'll master it."

"This is for you." Nora handed Adam a legal-sized manila envelope.

He withdrew the documents, scanned them, then looked up sharply.

"This is the deed to the chalet. I don't understand."

Nora watched his face. "You've always loved this place. I wanted you to have it."

"But it's ours, Mother. Yours and mine. Why would you give it to me?"

"Adam," she said patiently, "everything I own will be yours when I die. But I wanted the pleasure of giving you this gift now. This chalet has always been special to us."

As he made a move to protest, she held up a hand. "Please indulge me, Adam."

Placing the documents back in the envelope, he bent and kissed her. "Thank you, Mother. You know I'll treasure it."

Lounging on the floor by the fireplace, B.J. sipped her brandy, feeling the love and warmth shared by these people spread through her. Whatever heartache had been in their lives, there had also been much love.

Adam sat down beside B.J. and dropped a large package in her lap.

"What's this?"

"Open it." He appeared solemn, but his eyes were warm as they studied her.

She stared at the package for long moments and ran her hands over it as if afraid it would disappear. Then, tearing the bright paper from the box, she lifted the lid. Moving aside the tissue, she let out a gasp. Without warning, tears sprang to her eyes.

"Oh, Adam." Gently, almost reverently, she picked up the antique doll. "Oh, Adam." The tears spilled over, running down her cheeks.

Unable to find the words, she hugged the doll to her heart, then wrapped her arms around Adam's shoulders and buried her wet face against his neck. For a moment he sat motionless. Then, feeling the tremors she sought to hide from the others, he drew her into his arms and held her until she grew still. He lifted her face and wiped her tears with his thumbs.

"There's a child hidden deep inside each of us," he murmured against her temple. "Mother has a great need to be self-sufficient, to prove something to herself, or perhaps to her long-dead mother. So she demands her independence. I have a need, every now and then, to come back here, to see the place that was always my anchor, and gave me so much happiness as a boy." His warm voice washed over her, causing her tears to flow again. "If I had it in my power, Jess, I'd give you everything you ever missed as a child."

The logs in the fireplace glowed red. The festive candles burned low. The mountains and forests beyond the windows were swallowed in the blackness of night. Wrapped in a hazy glow, Nora kissed each member of her party good night. Leaning heavily on Martin's arm, she made her way upstairs.

"Come on, Jess." Adam helped her up, and noted with a smile that she still carried the doll in her arm. In her other hand dangled her shoes.

They made their way past the pool and sauna, to their private quarters. They stopped at her door.

"I'll never forget this," B.J. murmured.

Adam stared down at her, loving the warm contentment that softened her features. With a finger, he touched her face. "Your cheeks are hot."

"It's the fire. Or the brandy. I probably had too much of both."

His fingertips grazed her jaw, then moved lower, to the pulse beat that throbbed at her throat. It leaped at his simple touch.

"I'd better get the door for you." He swung it open, then took her shoes from her hand and set them on the floor of the closet.

B.J. placed the doll on her dresser and studied it for long, silent moments.

She looked up to see Adam watching her in the mirror. As she watched he walked closer, until he was standing directly behind her. In the mirror she saw his arms come around her waist. She tried to steel herself against the current that began flowing as soon as he touched her. His head bent until his lips were brushing her hair.

"You didn't take notes."

Her eyes widened. "What?"

He chuckled, and the sound was warm and muffled against her hair. "Tonight. Dinner, the monastery, the exchange of gifts. You didn't take any notes."

She turned in his arms. Meeting his laughing eyes, she said, "What makes you think I'm not going to start jotting them down right now?"

"You're not." The gruff tone of his voice sent tremors tingling along her spine. He brushed a strand of hair from her cheek. His fingertips traced the curve of her cheek to her jaw.

B.J. swallowed. "Why?"

"Because I'm not going to let you." He took the jeweled comb from her hair and watched as the thick waves tumbled about her neck and shoulders.

"And just how are you going to stop me?" Something tightened inside her.

"I'm going to keep you too busy to think about your manuscript tonight. We have better things to think about." He plunged his hands into her hair and drew her close.

"Adam..." Her words were cut off by the pressure of his lips on hers.

With his hands cupping both sides of her face, he kissed the corner of her mouth, her cheek, her temple, her eyelids. She closed her eyes, loving the feel of his lips on her skin. His breath had the sharp tang of brandy. On his clothes lingered the faint scent of woodsmoke from the fireplace. His skin had the clean, fresh scent of evergreen. Her lids fluttered open. She stared up into those gray eyes that had once seemed as cold as steel. Now she saw warmth in them, and desire.

His arms came around her, drawing her close. She wrapped her arms around his waist and brought her lips to his throat.

She felt his sudden intake of breath. His arms tightened around her. "Jess."

She looked up. "What?"

He kissed the tip of her nose. "Do you know what you want yet?" He kissed her chin, then dipped his mouth to the hollow of her throat.

Arching herself in his arms, she thrilled to the tiny sensations that fluttered deep inside her at his touch. His hands roamed her back, molding her to him. Her body was soft against his and she wanted to melt into him.

He brought his lips lower, to her collarbone. His hands moved up her sides until his thumbs found her breasts. Over the silk he traced the swollen outline. Need ripped through her, shattering her last threads of control.

Clutching his head, she brought his lips to hers. The kiss was hot, hungry. Still his thumbs continued to stroke her until a moan escaped her lips.

"Tell me, Jess." He spoke against her lips. "Tell me."

She hadn't realized how hard it would be to speak. The words felt lodged in her throat. In a faltering rasp she moaned inside his mouth, "I want you, Adam."

He crushed her to him. Their kiss became a desperate, pulsing need, taking them beyond thought. She clung to him, afraid that her legs would no longer support her.

Frustrated by the restriction of her dress, his hands moved at her back. Caught up in a frenzied desire, B.J. was hardly aware of his fingers gliding the zipper down, and her dress whispering to the floor. Then she was in his arms, and he strode through the dressing room to the massive bed in his room.

He was beyond thought. He didn't remember shedding his clothes. He knew only a need so desperate, a hunger so deep, nothing except this woman could satisfy his longing. He had wanted this to be a tender moment. But the minute he lay beside her, and took her in his arms, tenderness fled. It was replaced by an almost savage intensity.

"God, Jess, you're even more beautiful than I'd dreamed." His gaze burned over her, as if memorizing every detail of her body.

She lay on her side, with one knee slightly bent. His fingertips traced her knee, then glided upward along her thigh, to the flare of her hips. His palm opened at her slender waist, as if measuring her to his hand span. With his hand still open, he slid it upward to the swell of her breast, and watched her eyes darken at his touch.

She reached for him, drawing him to her. Her fingertips encountered a scar, raised and knotted in the flesh of his shoulder.

"What's this?" Her fingers traced the outline.

"From the accident. It doesn't hurt anymore. It's just there, a reminder of the war." His voice deepened. "I carry a lot of scars, Jess."

He bent his lips to the taut nipple, and heard her little moan of pleasure. His lips journeyed over her body, teasing, tempting, until she writhed with a pulsing need.

"Adam." She wasn't certain if she spoke his name or only thought it.

For a moment he lifted his head. Then his lips covered hers in a searing kiss. Now she was his; he was hers. He was in her; in every part of her. His breath was hot, shaky, his scent dark and musky. Even his heartbeat resounded in her chest, keeping rhythm to her own erratic beat. They were one, merging, separating, then merging again.

She clung to him, matching his strength, his movements.

"Jess." He felt a kind of madness drive him. Her scent, her taste were all he was aware of. He had lost himself completely in her. "Stay with me, Jess. Let me take you. Come with me, Jess."

His madness gripped her as well. Some of her was Adam now. And some part of herself would never be the same.

The tempo of their lovemaking increased, until they were beyond thinking. There was only hot, consuming need.

Together, they soared, exploded, then drifted weightless through space.

Spent, Adam buried his damp face against her throat. His breathing was as ragged as hers. Still united, they clung, terrified to release their tenuous hold.

"Cold?"

"Umm. No." Naked, she lay beside him, snuggled under a down quilt.

"I think I'll light a fire in the fireplace." Still he didn't move, reluctant to leave her.

"All right. As long as you're volunteering, I do think it's cold in here."

"But not so cold you're willing to get up and do anything about it." He grinned down at her.

"That's right."

He tossed back the quilt and crossed the room to the fireplace, stacked with logs. With some kindling, he started the fire.

Pulling back a corner of the drape, he commented, "Still dark outside. Want some champagne? It's still Christmas Eve."

"Do you have some?"

He pulled on a pair of velour sleep shorts. "Be back in a minute."

He returned with a silver tray laden with a bottle of champagne, two glasses and a plate heaped with cold meats, cheese, and crackers.

"You'll get crumbs in the bed," she muttered as he popped the cork.

"Then we'll eat on your side." He poured two glasses and handed one to her.

"Nice guy. Then I'll just have to sleep on your side."

He grinned. "Suits me. That's the way I planned it."

"Always thinking, aren't you?"

He kissed her nose. "I'll take any advantage I can."

"So you've told me." She plumped the pillows behind her, then tucked a sheet around her as she sat up. Her voice softened. "I loved spending Christmas with you and your mother, Adam. It's been a wonderful holiday."

"Do you have any family, Jess?" He waited, wondering if he had the right to pry, hoping she would answer.

She went very still. "An aunt. She lives in my mother's old house in New Jersey. A few cousins."

"No sisters or brothers?"

She shook her head.

"Tell me about your parents." He sat on the edge of the bed, facing her. He knew her body intimately. Now he wanted to know all of her.

She stared down into her glass. "There isn't much to tell. My mother died last year. My father died when I was ten."

"Were you close to them?"

She met his eyes and shrugged. "There was never time. My father was a Navy pilot. He was always being shipped off to another base. My mother and I would follow."

So, he thought grimly. She had firsthand knowledge of military service.

"And your mother?" He watched her eyes, seeing the pain of the memories reflected there.

"She seemed to save everything for my father. She only came alive when he was around. The rest of the time"—B.J. looked away—"she seemed to live in some dreamworld. There wasn't room for me in there."

"How did your father die?"

B.J. stared at Adam. Her eyes looked greener than he'd ever seen. "He was flying helicopters in Vietnam. His term of duty was up. He called to say he'd volunteered for one more mission. He wouldn't be home till Christmas."

Her voice lowered. She shivered and set her glass on the night table. "I'm cold, Adam."

"Here." He handed her a velour robe.

She kneeled up in bed to slip it on, then walked to the fireplace. With her back to Adam she stared at the flames.

For long moments he watched her. On the mantel, a clock chimed the hour.

Breaking the silence, he asked the question, although he thought he knew the answer.

"Did he make it home for Christmas?"

She turned. Her voice was a monotone, to bury the pain. "Yes."

Adam was surprised.

"We met the plane. I remember standing there, shivering in the cold. I'd forgotten my mittens.

And my mother had other things on her mind. I didn't want to tell her how cold I was. My mother stood very straight, for my father's sake. She didn't want to look weak and frail in front of all those military men.''

Adam watched her. She looked lost in his big robe. ''Go on, Jess.''

''And then all the men saluted. And my mother and I just stood there and watched as my father's casket was brought from the plane and carried to a waiting hearse.''

''Oh, my God.'' Adam stood, berating himself. He should have known. Now, at last, he understood why she hated war.

She rushed on, needing to tell him. ''After that my mother stayed in that other world. She laughed over jokes they'd shared. Jokes I didn't understand. Her eyes lit up whenever she spoke of him. She kept his uniforms in her closet. And she spent the rest of her life telling me how proud I should be that my father gave his life for his country.'' Her eyes filled. Tears glittered on her lashes, then spilled over, streaming down her cheeks. With an angry motion, she wiped them away. Her voice grew deep with controlled rage. ''How can I be proud of the fact that he would rather be part of that war than be home with us?''

In swift strides Adam crossed the room and gathered her in his arms. She held herself rigid, fighting the anger and revulsion she'd stored up through the years.

"Let it go, Jess," Adam murmured against her hair. "Now that you've finally said it out loud, finish it. Let the tears wash it all away."

"I don't want to cry. I want to scream. I want to tell the world how ugly war is."

His touch was tender, his words gentle. "Then do it. But first let it all go. Cry it out."

"Oh, Adam." Her voice was a cry of pain. Shudders wracked her slender body. With his arms holding her firmly against him, she clung to his waist and buried her face against his shoulder. Then she wept until she was exhausted.

Adam was overcome with a tenderness he'd never felt before. Her grief became his. He longed to take her pain away. Silently he stroked her hair and held her until the shudders subsided. Some scars, he thought with sudden insight, weren't visible. But they were just as real as the ones that crossed his back and shoulder, and ached at the oddest times.

When she grew quiet, Adam led her to the bed and poured some champagne. Handing her a glass, he murmured, "Thank you."

She glanced up at him. "For what?"

"For the gift you just gave me."

"What gift?"

He smiled and caught her hand. "The gift of trust. Ever since you came here, you've been learning all about my birth, my childhood, my whole life. But you've been a mystery. I know it wasn't easy for you to talk about yourself. And now that you have, I know you better."

Holding her hand between his, he studied her palm. "You have the hands of an artist. Long lean fingers. Sensitive." Lifting her palm, he pressed it to his lips. "You're a strong woman, Jess."

A flame began to flicker deep inside her.

Watching her eyes, he kissed each finger, then lifted her other hand to his lips.

She fought the fire inside her that began to rage out of control, heating her flesh, searing her mind.

"And your arms." He rolled the sleeves of the oversized robe and began dropping kisses on her wrist, the inside of her elbow. "I used to lie awake and dream of these arms around me." Taking her other arm, he pressed his lips to her wrist. He could feel the erratic beat of her pulse.

Desire rose in him, and he fought the urge to take her immediately. Their first time had been so intense, so all-consuming, they had come together in a raging storm. Now there was time to savor, to discover each other. He banked the needs that drove him, and forced himself to go slowly.

His hands moved to her shoulders. "You have an incredibly lovely throat, Jess." In one fluid motion he slid the robe from her shoulders and brought his lips to nuzzle the little hollow of her throat.

She shivered and drew him closer. "Do you know what you're doing to me?"

There was a gleam of triumph in his eyes. "I certainly hope so. Every advantage, remember, Jess?"

She gave a deep throaty laugh that ended in a groan as his lips moved lower to the swell of her breast. Lazily his tongue circled until her nipple grew taut. He caught it in his mouth, teasing, then moved to the other breast.

Wind danced down the mountains, rattling the windows, thrusting against the doors. Snow whirled in little gusts that sprayed against the house. Inside, snug and warm, B.J. drifted in a cocoon of pleasant sensations. Exhausted from her tears, sleepy from the champagne, she ran her hands through Adam's dark hair and drew his face to hers.

Her fingers trailed the muscles of his shoulders. Running a hand along the arm so recently encased in plaster, she was surprised to feel his strength. Her fingertips traced along his back and sides, then dipped lower. She felt his quick intake of breath, before he took the kiss deeper.

His hands and lips burned a trail of fire along her skin. There was no part of her he didn't explore. The journey was slow, torturous, as passion blazed out of control.

She no longer felt lethargic. Energy welled in her. She had an overpowering need to move with him, to touch him, to join him. Together they fell into a world of sensations. Their needs drove them to desperation.

With her arms around his waist, she drew him to her. She could no longer speak, to tell him of her needs. With a low moan of pleasure, she buried her mouth against his throat.

Adam knew he was no longer gentle. A madness had taken over his control once more. They had gone from one dizzying height to another. As his lips found her breast he felt her breath shuddering through her. He raised his mouth to hers once more.

To B.J. nothing mattered now except this man, this moment. She was his completely. If tomorrow they chose separate paths, at least they had this night. She moved with him, strong, drugged with power and passion. His name was torn from her lips, and then they were caught up in wave after shuddering wave, and all they could do was cling to each other wordlessly.

They slept, still locked in an embrace. When they woke, the first pale pink fingers of dawn streaked the sky.

Adam's lids fluttered. He found B.J. studying him. Lightly brushing his lips over hers, he murmured, "Good morning. Why the serious look?"

Her voice was hushed in the stillness of morning. "I woke up realizing that nothing's changed, Adam. What I'm writing might still hurt you. And I don't want to do that. But I'm committed to this book."

He felt the thrust of pain, swift, shocking. His lips brushed her temple. "I know, Jess. And I'm still going back to"—he sighed—"my dirty little war." He drew her closer. His deep voice, spoken against her lips, sent slivers of ice along her spine. "We won't think about it. For a little while we can have this."

Stifling her protest, his mouth covered hers in a burning kiss. Her arms came around his waist. Their bodies, naked, tangled in the sheets, warmed. Desire surfaced. And then all their fears were once more pushed aside by their loving.

Chapter Nine

B.J. awoke to the sound of bells. Sleigh bells
trilled on the frosty air as a horse-drawn sled
passed the chalet, then faded away as it moved
past. The carillon bells of dozens of churches
echoed through the mountains, then resounded
in the village below. Bells, she thought. The bells
of heaven. Her lids fluttered, whispering against
Adam's rough, scratchy cheek. He lay on his
stomach, with his face touching hers. His arm
was thrown protectively across her, holding her
to him.

As she started to move, his hand tightened,
pulling her firmly against him.

"Don't go. You feel so good here."

"I'm not going anywhere. I just wanted to re-kindle the fire."

"How about lighting mine." He nuzzled her throat and felt the warmth of a chuckle deep in her throat as she relaxed against him.

"You're incorrigible."

"No. Insatiable." He wrapped her in a warm embrace and was stunned at the rush of feelings. He'd never known a woman who could arouse him with a single word, a touch. He'd never have enough of her. Never.

"What do you usually do on Christmas Day?" she asked, breaking through his thoughts.

He leaned up on one elbow and traced her lips with his finger. "Shave, shower, get dressed, find a place that serves a decent breakfast."

"I mean when you're here with your mother."

He grinned. "I know what you mean. Gerta will prepare a breakfast fit for royalty. Then Mother, Flynn and Martin will take Gerta to her niece's and spend the day visiting friends in the village. Everyone here loves my mother. These people are like family. And with Gerta gone to-night, they'll have dinner at the village inn."

"Will we be expected to join them?"

He smiled and brushed his lips over hers. "I have other plans for us." He kissed her lightly, almost lazily.

B.J. ran a fingertip along his back and felt his arms tighten around her. Then the kiss deep-ened, until she felt her universe begin to tilt at a crazy angle. She was amazed at the feelings that washed over her at his simple touch.

"What plans?" Her throaty voice was warm with laughter.

"These." With his tongue, he traced her full lower lip. Nipping, he tugged on it with his teeth, until her lips trembled to be kissed. He took the kiss deeper, savoring the taste of her. Moving his mouth along her throat, he inhaled the musky morning sweetness of her.

"We should go down to breakfast."

"Not yet. I'm still hungry for you." His lips moved along her throat. He traced her collarbone with his tongue. Delicious swirls of pleasure enveloped her. His mouth continued its journey until it found her breast. He felt her trembling response.

"I feel like a man making up for lost time," he murmured against the smooth skin of her stomach.

Or one storing up memories for the future, she thought with a stab of pain. She tried desperately to change the course her thoughts were taking. But the fact was, her book was nearly completed. His wounds had healed enough to allow him to go back to Central America. These wonderful days in Gstaad were a prelude to parting.

His mouth dipped lower, and she gasped, shutting out all thought. His tongue drove her to a point of frenzy, until she clutched at him with a feeling of desperation. He raised his head and covered her lips in a hungry kiss.

Rays of brilliant sunshine, reflected off the snow, streamed through a narrow part in the drapes, bathing the figures in the bed with an iridescent glow. Through narrowed eyes, he studied her, loving the way her hair looked, tumbled and tangled on his pillow.

Watching him, she moved her hands along the flat plane of his stomach. When she touched him, she heard his gasp of pleasure. With a desperate need, they came together, each giving more than they had ever dreamed they possessed, each taking until they were sated.

While Adam showered, B.J. pulled on his robe and walked from the bed, intent on going to her own room. A series of framed photographs on his desk stopped her. She paused to study them.

There were over a dozen pictures. All were children. Though they were obviously taken in a wide variety of countries, there was a similarity to each of them. Some of them were maimed, some whole. But all had the hollow faces and vacant eyes of children who had witnessed the horrors of war and survived it, only to go through it endlessly in their dreams.

Hearing the shower stop, B.J. replaced the last photo and hurried to her room. She stripped off Adam's robe and waited until she heard him leave their adjoining bathroom, then entered, stepped beneath the stinging spray, and thought about Adam's job.

How could he see the suffering, and then return to this life of luxury? And once home, how could he freely choose to face returning to the rigors of war once more?

She had been wrong about Adam London. He wasn't trying to glorify the killing. And he was too private a person to use this job as a stepping stone to fame. He had known fame, or infamy, since birth.

Maybe he was sincere in wanting to educate the world about the evils of war. She turned off the taps and draped herself in a bath sheet. Knowing that Adam's intentions were honorable didn't change anything. She still hated his job. And there was no way she could willingly watch someone she loved go back to a war.

Love. The thought left her stunned and reeling. She didn't love Adam. She couldn't afford to. They had gone into this with their eyes open. It could go no further than this. Especially with the complications in their lives. But the tiny thought nagged and grew until it became a word on her lips. Love. *My God, how I love him.*

"We're going to the village after breakfast. Would you like to join us?"

Nora was dressed in a hand-knit sweater and skirt, with fur-trimmed boots that reached her knees. Her eyes seemed almost too large for her pale face. On her cheeks were two bright spots of color.

B.J. continued to drink her coffee, while Adam answered for both of them.

"Sorry, Mother. Jess and I are going skiing."

B.J.'s head came up sharply. He hadn't said a word about it.

"I don't blame you." Nora glanced out the window. "It's a perfect day for it. Will you join us for dinner at the inn?"

"We'll try. But don't wait for us. You know what the crowds will be like today."

Gerta entered with trays of poached eggs, thick slabs of rare roast beef, and steaming pastries, still warm from the oven.

With relish, B.J. began sampling Gerta's wonderful cooking. Today the cares of the world were forgotten. Today, she would ski with Adam and pretend that tomorrow would never come. For this one day they were simply a man and a woman who had discovered something rare and wonderful.

When the sleigh came to take the others to the village, B.J. hurried to her room to dress for a day on the slopes. Outside, Adam loaded their skis on a rented BMW.

Within an hour they were headed for the tram that would take them high into the Alps. B.J. moved beside Adam through the crush of bodies crammed into the lift. Maneuvering their skis, they moved to the window. Pressed against the glass in the crowded gondola, B.J. stared in awe.

"Close your mouth, Jess."

She turned to glance at Adam and burst into laughter. "What are they called?" She pointed.

"The sheer slope is the Schlaukhorn and the jagged peaks are the Spitzhorn."

"I can't believe this." She shook her head. "I'm actually going to spend the day on these storybook mountains."

"I forgot to ask. Can you ski?"

She arched one eyebrow. "It's a little late for that, isn't it?"

"Well, do you? Or do I have to take you down on my back?"

"I'll manage. Of course, my backside will probably be soaked by the time we make it to the bottom. But don't worry, Mr. London. I'll make it if you do."

She touched the bulge at his chest. "I know you got rid of the cast. What's this, a flask of brandy for the weary traveler?"

He opened his jacket. "My camera. I want pictures of you, Jess."

"Gracefully sprawled in the snow, I suppose?"

He grinned. "If you fall, I'll catch you."

"Um-hmm. After you've snapped the picture, I'll bet."

The cable car ground to a halt, and the crowds filed onto the slopes.

The sun reflecting off the snow was so brilliant that it was impossible to look at it without sunglasses. Adjusting their skis, they stood at the summit, watching the blur of color against the pristine background as dozens of skiers started down the mountain.

"Jess."

She turned. Adam touched the motor drive and squeezed off several shots before she realized what he was doing.

"You could have warned me you were going to take my picture."

"Then you'd look posed. I want to capture the real you, Jess, not some idea of what you think you should look like."

"You mean like this?" She made a terrible face and heard the whir of the camera.

"Perfect. It's you."

"Oooh." With her hands on her hips, she would have stomped her feet, but they were encased in skis. Instead she crossed her eyes and stuck out her tongue as he aimed the camera again.

"Good show."

"Come on." She turned and hovered at the edge of the slope. "Bet I beat you down."

He zipped the camera inside his jacket and picked up his ski poles.

"You're on."

At the top of the slope she stayed ahead of Adam, leaving a trail in the fresh snow. But as they neared a stand of evergreens, her ski caught the edge of a boulder, and she sprawled face down in the snow.

Adam was beside her instantly. After quickly releasing his skis, he caught her by the arm and lifted her to a sitting position.

"Are you hurt?"

She brushed the snow from her face and gave him a weak smile. "Just my ego."

"You're sure you're okay?"

She nodded. "Really. I'm fine."

"I'll collect your skis in a minute." Opening his jacket, he brought the camera to his eye.

Her hair looked like it had the first time he'd met her. Against the dazzling snow it was lush and wind-tossed. Her cheeks that first time had been flushed from the fire, or maybe from his angry scrutiny. Now their color came from the glow of health and the frosty air. Her green eyes danced with mischief. With great concentration, he touched the button and managed several shots before the snowfall splattered on his cheek.

His head shot up.

"I knew you'd take advantage of this." Her laughter rippled on the clear air.

"Oh. You want to play, do you?"

In one swift movement he swung the camera from his neck, dropped it on his skis, and lunged toward her. Evading his grasp, she rolled to one side and tossed another handful of snow. It caught him on the back of the neck.

"That one will cost you, lady." His hand snaked out, catching her by the ankle.

She tried to stand, but with a tug he brought her down beside him.

"Think you're smart, don't you?" He straddled her, then scooped up a handful of snow and held it menacingly over her.

"This is for the surprise attack," he muttered, releasing a fine spray of snow that trickled over her cheeks, causing her to shake her head to avoid him.

"And this is for that deadly aim," he said with a laugh, allowing the snow to trickle down the collar of her ski parka.

"Adam, I'm freezing!"

"Couldn't happen to a nicer person."

"Come on. You've had your revenge. Let me up."

"In a minute." His voice deepened. His fingertips brushed the snow from her cheek.

She saw his eyes darken as they fastened on her mouth. "God, you're lovely, Jess. I want to remember you this way always."

She hadn't expected the pain to be so sharp. Was Adam afraid he'd forget what she looked like? Was that why he insisted on these pictures today? She studied his face. She would never forget him. Years from now she would be able to close her eyes and trace that proud forehead, those gray eyes that could be so brooding, or so tender. She would always be able to feel the softness of his lips against hers.

He bent closer until his lips were brushing hers. "This time next year, when I'm in some godforsaken jungle, I'll take out these pictures and remember this." His lips covered hers in a searing kiss. Their breath mingled, rising like a single mist on the frigid air.

His hands tangled through her hair, and he pressed her body close to his. The kiss deepened. He lifted his head and brushed his lips across her cheek, then kissed her eyelid. His head came up sharply.

"Is that a tear, Jess? Are you crying?"

Angrily she brushed the moisture from her eye. "It's just the cold. It always makes my eyes water. Come on. I can still beat you."

Standing, she turned away to avoid his scrutiny. Furiously she brushed away the snow, then adjusted her skis and started down the slope, never once looking back to see if Adam was following.

When they paused on the crest of a hill, Adam playfully tugged her hair. "Eyes still tearing? You can borrow my goggles if you'd like."

"No, thanks. I have my own." She studied the sheer mountain wall.

Adam's voice lowered beside her. "I'm glad we had this time. I'll never forget it. Or you."

She steeled herself to meet his steady look. "I'm glad too, Adam. And I'll never forget you either."

His voice became a monotone, to deny the pain he felt. "We touch a lot of people in this life. and then we move on."

"Yes." The lump in her throat was threatening to choke her. She shivered.

"Come on." His voice was suddenly gruff. "We have a long way to go yet."

"Do we?"

His gaze held hers. "Yes."

They started off more slowly, as if reluctant to reach the end of their journey.

Adam crept from the bed and pulled on a pair of faded jeans. A full moon, reflecting off the snow, bathed the room in opaque light. For long minutes he stared at the sleeping figure of the woman in his bed. They had eaten dinner at a wonderful old inn, surrounded by boisterous holiday skiers. Then, relieved to be rid of the party scene, they had hurried back to the chalet, where their lovemaking had been as passionately intense as the first time. They had clung to each other as if afraid to let go. They were both aware, he thought, watching her steady breathing, that this idyll must come to an end.

A smile touched his mouth. Jess would be stiff and sore in the morning from the strenuous skiing. Her muscles weren't accustomed to this.

Touching his arm gingerly, he winced. Neither were his. The doctor had warned him the arm would be weakened from such prolonged inactivity. He drew on a flannel shirt and rolled the sleeves above his elbows.

With a last glance at Jess he turned and made his way to the small darkroom at the end of the hall. Opening the door, Adam felt the familiar warmth he always felt upon entering this room. Josh had had this installed years ago. He had patiently taught a very young Adam the intricacies of film developing. Adam smiled to himself as he moved deftly about the room. Josh Thompson's brilliance as a director was renowned; his genius as a photographer was largely ignored.

A short time later Adam watched the figure begin to take shape on the print. He smiled as she swam before his eyes, then came into sharp focus.

After hanging the picture, he took a step back to study it. The camera had captured her hair, lush and dark against the mound of snow. Her eyes were laughing. He had noticed that humor in their very first encounter, at his mother's apartment in New York. And he had caught the intelligence as well.

Jess knew that their lives took very different routes. From the beginning she had been intelligent enough to know that neither of them would agree to a commitment. His fists clenched at his sides. He had known it from the beginning as well. Still, now that it was almost time to consider going back to work, he found the thought of separation too painful. He hadn't expected it to hurt like this.

She meant more to him than any woman he had ever known. Wherever he went, whatever he did, he would always wonder about her; whether she was eating enough; whether the book she was writing would be well received; whether her life was as fulfilling as she deserved. He felt a knife-thrust near his heart. Whether someone else was holding her, loving her.

The next print came into focus. Her eyes were crossed. She had stuck out her tongue at the camera. He chuckled. She was crazy. Absolutely crazy. And he loved her.

He gripped the edge of his work table. Love. Love meant sharing your life; it meant caring about the one you love so much, you'd die rather than hurt her. All his life he had religiously avoided emotional entanglements. Like his mother, he thought grimly, he would rather have life on his own terms. He wasn't a man who liked compromise. And love would sometimes demand giving in. Besides, his work was important to him. Despite his loathing for the killing, he endured it because his pictures graphically showed the world the dark side of war.

Love. He shook his head and hung another picture. In this one she was pensive, staring at the sheer cliffs that rose majestically to the clouds. Her lips were full, inviting. Her eyes were ringed with a thick fringe of lashes that had feathered across his face like the whisper of a butterfly. It was heaven waking up with her in his arms. If he could, he would keep her with him always. If he could. He began to smile as he continued his work. It was a tempting thought.

When Adam worked in the darkroom, he lost all concept of time. The knock on the door pulled him from his reverie. Had he been here hours, or just a short time? He glanced at his watch, surprised by the lateness of the hour. He quickly hung the last prints, and turned the handle of the door.

"Flynn. What's wrong?"

His mother's secretary was wrapped in a quilted bathrobe. Her dark hair, always neatly pinned back, fell in wild disarray about her shoulders. The eyes beneath the glasses were puffy from sleep.

"It's your mother, Adam. She's—very ill. Martin is on the phone, trying to get us back to New York as quickly as possible."

"Back to New York?" Without a thought to the work behind him, he rushed past her and began hurrying toward his mother's room. "Are you crazy? If she's sick, she can't possibly make that trip. Have you called a doctor?"

"Adam." Flynn touched his sleeve, and he whirled.

Seeing her grim expression, he hesitated.

"This isn't a sudden illness," she said softly.

"I don't understand."

"She'll want to tell you herself."

He gripped her arms, unaware of his strength. "No. You'll tell me. Now."

She gasped, more surprised than hurt. "She's been—fighting an illness for a long time now. That's why she insisted on going to New York. She's been getting treatments there at a famous medical center."

"Then why the sudden decision to fly to Gstaad?"

Flynn looked away, unwilling to meet his gaze. "Please, Adam. You're hurting me."

He dropped his hands and waited for her to continue.

"I'd like you to hear this from her."

"No. From you. I'm waiting, Flynn. Why did she make this trip?"

She expelled her breath in a long sigh. "Because she wanted to see it all one last time."

"One last time."

In the silence that followed, she said softly, "Hurry now, Adam. She wants to talk to you before we begin the long journey home."

Without another word, Adam walked across the enclosed pool area and entered the main house. As he made his way to his mother's room, his fists clenched and unclenched in silent rage.

Just as he reached the door to his mother's room, it opened. B.J. emerged, her hands thrust deeply into the pockets of his oversized robe.

"Jess, what?..."

"Oh, Adam. Your mother asked for me. But it's you she really wants to see. Please hurry. There are so many things she has to tell you."

His eyes narrowed. A dozen questions came to mind, but he swallowed them back. Right now the only thing that was important was his mother's health. Once he was satisfied that she was all right, he'd deal with other things.

"I'm going to pack now."

"Pack?" Adam found himself wondering how she could think of such inane things at a time like this.

"Nora wants to return to New York. She's determined to find a flight out tonight."

Impatient, he strode past her and into his mother's room. "We'll see about this."

Nora's voice, weaker than it had ever sounded before, could be heard in the room. "Oh, Adam, I should have told you. But I wanted to spare you as long as possible. Sit here beside me. There's so much I have to explain."

B.J. watched with troubled eyes as the door swung shut behind him. Turning, she saw Gerta standing in the hallway, her hands gripped together in an attitude of paralyzing fear.

"Gerta." Flynn moved purposefully along the hall. "See that Miss London's things are packed and ready to go within the hour."

Glad for something to do, the maid nodded and hurried to her task.

To B.J., Flynn said, "Martin has located a flight. I've already sent for transportation." As if to herself, she muttered, "The whole town will know something is wrong. We've always traveled by sleigh here, until tonight."

She glanced up and seemed to catch herself. "Did you get the tape?"

B.J. pulled the cartridge from her pocket. "Right here. Nora said she had spoken as much as she could think of into the tape recorder."

"She instructed me to answer any questions you might have."

"Oh, Flynn." B.J. sighed in frustration at this strange turn of events. It was all too much, too soon. She didn't seem able to take it all in. "What can I do?"

The secretary paused for a moment, her dark eyes fixed on the young woman she had so recently feared. "Do you know how to pray?"

Alone in her room, B.J. dressed and packed. When her luggage was closed and waiting, she opened the drapes and watched the first soft light of dawn on the horizon. Wearily she sat down in a chair and turned on the tape recorder.

It was odd to hear that now familiar voice speaking to her in the semidarkness.

"There were so many things I wanted to tell you myself. I know that you can get my movie credits from a number of reference books. But my personal life is another story, Jessica. I want to explain about Adam's father.''

In the hush of dawn, watching the sky blush just above the tallest mountain peaks, B.J. sat alone and listened as the velvet tones of Nora London washed over her, weaving a tale of love and heartbreak, ending a thirty-seven-year vow of silence.

When the tape ended, B.J. continued to sit in the shadows, listening to the soft whir of the machine.

She had her answers. And by now, Adam had them too. Finally he knew the name of his father. She hoped Nora had the strength to tell him everything.

B.J. looked up at the sound of drawers being slammed in the next room. Adam. She hurried to offer him comfort.

"Adam?" She stood in the doorway.

Earlier she had carefully folded his robe and placed it on his bed. Now it lay in a heap on the floor. His suitcases stood open. With quick gestures he dumped the contents of his closet into the bags without any concern for neatness.

"Here, let me help," she said, walking toward him.

"I don't need your help."

At his icy tone, she paused.

"Adam, I'm so sorry about your mother."

He turned to stare at her. "Are you? How long have you known that she was ill, Jess?"

"Just now. When you did, Adam."

"Really." His voice dripped sarcasm. "You've been spending so much time with her, I'm surprised the topic never came up."

"Flynn said she didn't want anyone to know."

"Including me."

B.J.'s voice lowered. "I know it seems cruel, Adam. I don't understand it either. But I'm sure she had her reasons."

"Just as she had her reasons for not telling me who my father was." He pinned her with his steely gaze. "She finally told me. When it's too late."

"But at least now you know."

He took a step toward her and caught her chin. "We don't have any secrets now, do we? You know, too, don't you, Jess?"

She froze.

He lifted her chin, forcing her to meet his look. "Don't you?"

"Yes." She swallowed.

"And you've known all along."

"No. I just—"

"It figures. The damned biography. It's more important than my feelings."

"Adam, let me explain."

"No." He felt too weary to move. "Just get out of here, Jess, and let me pack."

He turned away from her.

"I wasn't in your mother's bedroom to find out facts for the book. She sent for me just before you arrived. She just wanted to give me—"

"I don't want to hear." She saw the fire in his eyes, heard the edge to his tone.

She stood with her hands on her hips. "Well, that's too bad. You're going to hear it anyway. All you know is who your father was. But I know why. And it's critical that you know it, too. Otherwise the love and respect you have for those two people will be shattered."

He scooped up a handful of sweaters and dropped them in a suitcase. He walked to the bathroom and began tossing toilet articles in a zippered bag. When he emerged, he glanced at her, then moved past her.

His voice was toneless. "I have no complaints coming, Jess. Let's stop the arguing. We both knew what we were doing. Now it's over. I just want to get my mother back to her doctor for more treatments. And you have to get home and write that bestseller."

He supposed he'd always known it would come to this. From the beginning they knew their lives would take different courses. And he had tried to prepare himself for their parting. But he'd hoped for more time. And he was shocked at the depth of his pain.

For long moments she stared at his rigid back. If he would fight with her, she could handle it. What she couldn't take was his calm withdrawal from her. Without another word she slipped away to her room. She wasn't going to give up. She'd find a way to get through to him. Right now he needed some time. And some distance.

Chapter Ten

With Adam and Martin supporting her, Nora made her way slowly to the waiting limousine. B.J. rode with Gerta and Flynn in a second car.

"Why didn't you hire an ambulance?" B.J. asked quietly.

"No ambulance," Flynn snapped. "I won't have the townspeople staring at her and whispering. The last thing Nora ever wanted was to make a spectacle of herself. She was appalled at all the intrusions into her private life."

In the soft light of dawn the two cars slowly made their way down the hillside and through the still sleeping town.

B.J. watched the shuttered shops and gingerbread houses slip past the window. Rays of light from the rising sun cast their benediction on the snowcapped peaks of the Alps that surrounded the valley. B.J.'s heart was heavy. The ebb and flow of this village life had caught her up in its gentle rhythm. It was as if, in this brief time, all the things that had seemed to matter so much to her before had receded to the background. Success, fame, financial security were now empty goals. Even the book had taken on less meaning. What really mattered now? Adam. The thought crept unbidden to her mind. Adam's respect. Adam's trust. Adam's love.

Her heart contracted at the thought. She had promised Nora a fair, honest biography. And if she kept that promise, it would destroy what she and Adam had just begun to build.

She bit her lip to keep it from trembling, and turned to stare out the window. Tears blurred her vision.

At the train depot dozens of cars and sleighs awaited the arrival of the morning train. The two limousines parked at a discreet distance and waited until the passengers departed the station. With only a few scattered strangers loitering about, Adam and Martin assisted Nora to a private car. Flynn saw to the luggage while Gerta prepared tea and broth and took care of Nora's personal comfort.

By the time the train started on the first leg of their journey, Adam and Martin were huddled in a corner, their faces grim, their voices a low rumble over the steady rattle of the train. Gerta and Flynn kept a constant vigil at Nora's side, attuned to her slightest need. Alone, hunched in the corner of the bench, B.J. felt like a useless appendage. Occasionally Adam's gaze wandered to her. Instantly, he would look away, as if angry that his eyes had betrayed him. He scrupulously avoided speaking to her. The break had to be clean, he decided. It was the only way he could deal with it. Besides, he reasoned, it would take all his energy to cope with his mother's illness.

The short trip to Berne seemed an eternity. And the flight in the small plane to Gatwick Airport outside London was spent almost entirely in grim silence. Once their party boarded the 747 to New York, the atmosphere seemed, if not cheerful, at least less strained. The stewardess did everything possible to make the actress comfortable. The arrival of hot food did nothing to revive their spirits.

Adam and Gerta sat on either side of the actress, casting worried glances at her pale features. The strain of the difficult journey was evident in the tight lines about her mouth, the pallor of her skin. Adam grasped her hands. Despite the warm blanket, they were cold.

In the row behind them, Flynn stared out the small window of the plane. Except for her bleak expression, she gave no indication of her thoughts. Beside her, B.J.'s eyes were fixed on the top of Adam's dark head, barely visible above the cushion. Alongside B.J., Martin's hands gripped the arm rests. For once he had no amusing anecdotes, no hearty joke to bring a laugh. He chewed the end of an unlighted cigar until, in frustration, he stubbed it into an ashtray and rang for a drink.

"Did you know about this?" B.J. asked him.

He shook his head and drained his glass. "No. But it certainly explains a lot." He turned to meet her questioning gaze. "I couldn't figure out why Nora, after a lifetime of silence, would actually invite a writer to do her biography. Now I see the logic."

At B.J.'s arched eyebrow, he explained, "The press will get wind of this in a matter of days. There's just no way to keep this under wraps. And when they do, it will start again."

Martin glanced at Adam's head in the row ahead. "She knew this was coming. And for his sake, she wanted to end the rumors and gossip forever. With an authorized biography, all the facts will be laid bare." He stared into B.J.'s eyes, and for long moments their look held. "You know, don't you? She told you who Adam's father is."

She didn't speak. There was no need.

After what seemed an interminable silence, he nodded. "Good. Write the truth, Jessica. That's what she's always wanted. It can't hurt her—now."

B.J. heard the tone of resignation and turned away, fighting a cold lump of fear that settled around her heart.

When the plane landed in New York, Flynn efficiently handled everything. While their luggage was dispatched to the apartment, they were whisked to the hospital, where a private suite was already prepared. Waving aside a nurse's offer of help, Flynn personally prepared Nora for bed while the others waited in an antiseptic sitting room.

The doctor was brisk without being indifferent. Adam's voice went from cold fury to impatient acceptance of the facts. From the way Nora's doctor explained her illness to them, B.J. knew that he had been intimately involved in her treatment for a long period of time.

"How long does she have?" Adam's steel gaze pinned the doctor.

"We don't run on timetables here," the doctor replied sharply. Then, seeing the helplessness in those gray eyes, he added more softly, "It could be a matter of hours, or days. No more."

"I'll stay here," Adam said, glancing at the sofa bed.

"It's all been arranged." The doctor paused in the doorway. "I hope you understand that there are no more treatments we can offer. The only thing we can do now is make your mother comfortable.''

Adam nodded and turned away. Seeing the look of despair on his face, B.J. wanted to go to him and hold him and offer whatever comfort she could give. Instead, she glanced down at the floor, gripped her hands together tightly and did nothing.

When the doctor had finished his examination, Adam and Martin went to Nora's side. Martin kissed her goodbye and left the room. Watching him, B.J. saw an old man, his shoulders hunched, his lips trembling. Her heart ached for him.

Flynn emerged from Nora's bedroom, carrying her briefcase.

''We'll go now and leave Adam and Nora alone.'' She turned. ''Gerta, Miss London would like some of your famous chicken soup tonight.''

The old woman brightened and pulled herself from the leather chair, eager to do anything to ease her employer's burden. ''Good. I'll ask the driver to stop at the store and get what I need. Will I go in Mr. Stone's car?''

''If you'd like. Jessica and I will follow.''

As the old woman left the room, Flynn added, ''Nora probably won't be able to keep any food down, but she wanted Gerta to feel useful.''

It was typical, B.J. thought, of Nora London's kindness.

"Miss London would like you to stay on at the apartment while you finish the manuscript."

Firmly, B.J. shook her head. "No. If you don't mind, I'd like to go back to my place."

"But there may be questions you'll need answered," Flynn protested.

"Then I'll phone you." Her voice lowered. "I can't accept Nora's hospitality any longer. I think now I need to be alone while I finish my work."

Flynn nodded. "As you wish. If you have any questions..."

"There is one." B.J. bit her lip, then plunged on. "Why did Nora lie to me about giving an interview to Aubrey Madden?"

For a moment Flynn's dark eyes seemed to narrow behind the glasses.

"He knew about Adam's father, didn't he? And he threatened to tell in his column?" B.J. saw the eyes darken with anger.

"Do you really think Nora London could be blackmailed for such an unworthy reason?"

B.J. blinked. "Unworthy? She went to great lengths to keep her secret. If an unscrupulous man like Madden found out, it would take a great deal to keep him quiet."

"I thought you knew Nora London better than that, Jessica." Flynn's voice softened. "Nora would never resort to lies to save herself. But she would do anything to save her friends."

"What are you saying?"

"Sit down, Jessica." Flynn indicated the sofa.

B.J. sat, and Flynn nervously paced in front of her for long moments. Then she stopped and faced her. Her voice, when she spoke, was calm, determined.

"Nora London gave that interview for my sake."

"Your sake? I don't understand."

"Let me explain. In my own words. And please, don't interrupt."

B.J. nodded.

"I was thirty years old. I had worked for Nora London for seven long years. In that time I had an opportunity to travel around the world. I watched her cope with infamy, with a growing son, with people who adored her and people who tried to use her." She gave a grim smile. "At thirty, I thought of myself as a polished, sophisticated woman of the world. Nora London's personal secretary." A short little laugh escaped her lips. "Some sophistication."

At B.J.'s questioning look, she explained, "I met a man. Oh, I'd met a lot of them. But this one was different, I thought. He was so charming. He was a minor actor, on his way to becoming a star. How I loved him. And I think in the beginning he loved me, in his own way."

"What happened?"

Flynn stared at B.J. as if she had forgotten she was there for a moment. Her tone hardened. "He asked me to be there for him. He said his life in Hollywood would be tolerable only if he knew I'd always be there for him." She sighed. "Can you imagine how I felt? I was thirty years old. And I'd never loved anyone the way I loved him. And all he asked of me was that I be there for him. So I gave Nora my notice, and I moved into the apartment he bought me. For a while, we were so happy."

Her eyes misted over, and B.J. waited.

"Of course, there was one little thing he neglected to tell me."

"What was that?"

"That he was married."

At B.J.'s gasp Flynn looked down. "And by the time I finally found out, I was expecting his baby."

"Was he willing to get a divorce?"

Flynn gave a hard laugh. "It's such a classic story, Jessica. Not only did he not want a divorce, he didn't want a baby either. He arranged for a doctor he knew to take care of things." Her tone grew sharper. "Who knows. Maybe he'd had to face that sort of situation before. At any rate, the doctor took care of my—problem. And then afterward, when I became angry and depressed, the good doctor saw to it that I was supplied with plenty of medication to keep me from doing something foolish, like slitting my wrists or even crying the night away. There were pills to sleep, pills for the pain, pills to wake up in the morning." Flynn's voice became a flat monotone. "Some days I just didn't get out of bed at all. It was so pleasant to not have to think or do or care. And after his tender care, I was addicted to tranquilizers." Flynn looked past B.J., her gaze full of remembered pain. "Those were the lost years."

"Did the actor help you?"

"Are you joking? He went back to his wife as soon as he grew tired of me."

"Then how did you break the addiction?"

Her voice softened. Tears shimmered on her lashes. "Nora London heard about it. Even though I'd been gone for over four years, she hired a private investigator to find me. When he reported on my condition, she had me taken to a private hospital, where I stayed for six months. She paid for everything. When I was well enough to leave, she offered me my old job back. To this day, it has never been mentioned again."

At last B.J. had the reason for Flynn's five-year absence from Nora London's employ.

"What does this have to do with Aubrey Madden?"

Flynn's voice lowered with contempt. "He loved dirty little secrets. He thrived on them. When he found out that Nora London's former secretary was in a private hospital drying out, he began to dig deeper. When he found out the whole story, he called her and threatened to print it. Of course, that scandal would have destroyed the actor's marriage. And more important, Nora feared that the publicity would be too much for me to handle and that I would fall back into my addiction.''

At her words B.J. cringed. It was difficult to imagine this prim, fastidious woman addicted to prescription drugs.

Flynn continued, ''Nora asked Madden what it would take to buy his silence. The price he demanded was an exclusive interview with Nora London, complete with pictures of her and her son, Adam. At first, Nora refused to include Adam in the deal. When Adam heard, he insisted that she pay the price.'' Tears streamed down Flynn's face, smearing her makeup. ''All so that I'd be free of that scum, Aubrey Madden, for good.''

An oath exploded in the silent room. Both women turned to see Adam standing in the doorway.

''You're never satisfied, are you?'' Adam towered over them, scowling at B.J.

''Adam, I—''

He gave the secretary a quick glance. ''My mother wants you, Flynn.''

''But—''

''Now. Leave us.''

Wiping her eyes, Flynn hurried from the room. Adam stood, his hands on his hips, a look of fury darkening his face.

''You had to have it all, didn't you, Jess?''

''I don't know what you mean.''

"Everybody's deep, dark secrets. Mother's. Mine. Gerta's. And now Flynn's. What a great book you can write. A blockbuster. Sex. Drugs. A peek at the lives of the rich and famous. Just smile your way into our hearts and ask us to open up our veins and bleed all over your pages."

"Stop it, Adam."

His eyes narrowed. "And your timing is excellent. If Nora London will just cooperate now and die on cue, you can have that perfect best seller ready to roll."

"You bastard!" Her face went ashen.

In the silence of the room, she could hear her heart pounding against the wall of her chest. Even her breath seemed to have died in her lungs.

His voice, when he finally spoke, was flat. "Yes. That's what I've been all my life."

He turned on his heel and left her standing alone. For long minutes she stood rooted to the spot. The sound of monitors, the soft hiss of oxygen, were the only sounds coming from Nora London's suite. And then the sound of sobbing and hurried footsteps, as B.J. ran from the room.

"There were so many things I wanted to tell you. But I knew there wasn't time for everything. So I touched on some of the highlights. I'm not interested in facts and figures, Jessica. You can find those in your research. I'm interested in conveying the emotions that drove me.

Most of this can be verified in my diaries and journals.''

B.J. sat in the darkness of her cramped apartment and listened to the rich tones of Nora London, coming from the tape recorder.

''On this tape I want to talk about Adam's father. I mean really talk about him, as I haven't allowed myself to do in all these years. Oh, how I loved that man. I used to wonder if anyone else had ever known such passion. But as tormenting as that passion was, I loved him too much to allow our love to destroy what he had; what he was. He was so brilliant, so respected, so good. But the passion that caught us by surprise and snared us in its web would have shattered the lives of the people who mattered most to me, if it were ever to become public knowledge. And so I swore him to secrecy.''

All through the night she played the tapes, allowing the emotions of the actress to wash over her, to touch her. When at last the only sound in the early dawn was the soft scratching of the finished tape, B.J. stretched her cramped muscles and made a pot of tea. Then she walked to her typewriter and began to work.

NORA LONDON DEAD! Hollywood legend succumbs after long illness.

B.J. scanned the headlines, then read through the article carefully. It was as Martin had predicted. The old scandal was dredged up, and the speculations about Adam's father were carefully noted. Every man with whom Nora had ever worked was mentioned as a possible lover.

B.J. had phoned the hospital each day, to inquire about the actress's condition. No one except the immediate family was allowed to visit. The news had always been the same. Nora London was resting. B.J. covered her face with her hands. Now the actress had earned an eternal rest.

There would be no public memorial service, the newspaper stated. Her secretary revealed that the burial would be strictly private.

Fighting a feeling of lethargy, B.J. went back to her typewriter. Her head came up sharply at the sound of the telephone.

"Jessica, it's Flynn."

"Oh, Flynn. I just read the news. I'm so sorry."

The secretary's voice was raspy, as though she had been crying. "The service will be tomorrow. Adam wants it to be very small and private."

"How is he doing, Flynn?"

"He's—fine. Adam is accustomed to being alone, Jessica. He'll get over his anger in time." Her voice trembled for a moment. "I wonder if I did the right thing, keeping it from him for so long. But Nora was so determined."

"Flynn, don't blame yourself. I'll be there tomorrow." For a moment she didn't dare breathe. "And Flynn, thanks for calling me." B.J.'s voice sounded unnaturally bright. Her pulse rate accelerated. "Did Adam ask you to?"

There was an awkward pause.

"No. But I knew you'd want to be here."

B.J. took in a deep, painful breath. "Thank you."

B.J. stood under the street lamp staring at the lights at the top of the building. She'd been standing there for nearly an hour. She knew if she walked closer, the doorman would recognize her and lift his hat. Still she hesitated.

What would Adam say? At the funeral he had been proper and distant. When it was over, he had turned away without another word. There had been no word from him since.

Her hands inside the gloves felt stiff and frozen. The wind keened down the tall buildings, swirling snow showers against her red cheeks. She turned the collar of her coat up and hugged the manuscript to her chest. With a toss of her head she made her decision. There was no turning back.

At the entrance to Adam's apartment building, the doorman smiled and held the heavy door for her. Inside, she spoke to the security guard and asked him to announce her. Without waiting for his response, she headed for the elevator and pushed the button for the top floor.

Flynn was waiting for her when the elevator stopped.

"Jessica. What a surprise. I wasn't expecting you."

"How are you, Flynn?"

B.J. studied the woman she had come to respect. Her dark hair was pulled back in a severe bun; her tailored suit and crisp shirt were as fashionable as ever. But the eyes beneath the rimless spectacles were smudged with shadows.

"I'm a bit tired. We all are." She paused a moment, glancing at the manila envelope in B.J.'s hands. "Is there something I can do for you?"

B.J. nodded. "I'd like to see Adam."

Flynn looked down at the floor. "He isn't seeing anyone, Jessica."

"He'll see me."

The secretary shook her head firmly. "No. He won't."

"Where is he?"

"In the library."

"I'm going in there, Flynn. Don't try to stop me."

For a moment Flynn started to speak. Then, thinking better of it, she nodded. "Excuse me, Jessica. If he asks, tell Adam I've gone to my room."

B.J. waited until the secretary was gone before knocking on the library door.

"Come in."

She shivered at the sound of that deep voice. She opened the door and closed it softly behind her. There was a fire in the fireplace. A lamp on the desk was the only other source of light. In the shadowy light of the fireplace, Adam was seated on a leather sofa. As she entered he turned to study her.

His voice, when he finally spoke, sounded tired. "What do you want, Jess?"

"I wanted to see for myself that you were all right."

"You can see that I'm fine."

She moved closer. "And I wanted you to have this."

He stared at it, but made no move to accept it.

"At last," he said with venom. "The story of my life."

"No. Not yours, Adam. Your mother's."

"Get it out of here, Jess. I'm not interested. Take it to your publisher. I'm sure they can't wait."

"You have to read it, Adam." She had rehearsed this at home, but somehow it had been so much easier alone. Now, with Adam so near, her heart thudded in her chest. Her throat was parched. She had wanted him to understand, but now she was stumbling over the words.

She bit her lip. "I know you resent me. I know you think your mother told me things she'd never told you. And you're right. But not the way you think. The night that she took sick at the chalet, she gave me tapes."

She saw his eyes widen. Determined to hold his interest, she blurted, "That's why she gave me the tape recorder for Christmas. She had already begun making tapes of things she wanted me to know. But it was all for your sake. Don't you see? She knew what the gossip mongers would do when she died. She wanted the record set straight for you." B.J.'s voice softened. "I've played them over and over. And they're in here, along with the completed manuscript. I want you to listen to them. And I want you to read the book."

"No." He stood and turned his back on her. "I have no intention of giving my blessing on this scheme. Take your book and your tapes, Jess, and grab all the fame you can get. But don't ask me to give my approval."

"Don't you see, Adam?" she pleaded. "You, of all people, need to read this."

"Do you think I need you to explain my mother to me?"

"No. Not to explain. You know now who your father was. But I know why. And until you read this manuscript, you won't understand what really happened."

Her voice lowered. She turned toward the crackling fire. "Just read this. If you don't approve of it, if you think it in any way demeans your mother's life, or yours, then you have the right to destroy it." She walked to the door. With her hand on the knob, she turned. He continued to stare at the fire.

"I give it to you, Adam. It's yours, to do with as you please. Even if that means burning it."

Without another word, she left.

Chapter Eleven

B.J. sipped lukewarm coffee and paced the floor of her kitchen. She had slept badly. Had Adam read the manuscript, or had he simply tossed it in the fire without bothering to read a word of it?

She understood his anger, and yet she was stung by it. Hadn't they both gone into this with their eyes open? Hadn't they both known from the beginning that their relationship had no future? Then why this pain? Why the terrible ache each time she thought of him?

In frustration she berated herself. She was on the verge of having everything she had ever wanted, and she had just thrown it all away. The book was good. It would have made her wealthy and famous. But somehow, that didn't seem to matter anymore. And like a lovestruck fool, she had given it to Adam to destroy.

All night she had anticipated a phone call. Adam would tell her the book was wonderful, and he wanted it published in his mother's memory. Now, in the harsh light of morning, she realized what she had done. She had gambled everything on love. She had thrown away her future. And she had lost Adam in the bargain.

Why had she let him into her life? It had been so much easier before this. Until Adam, she had put all thoughts of love and marriage on hold. First she would build a successful career. Then she would find the perfect mate. What she hadn't counted on was falling in love with the wrong man.

The phone rang. B.J.'s heart stopped. She rushed to answer it, then froze. It rang a second time. A third. Her hand trembled on the instrument.

"Hello."

Her voice felt strangled in her throat.

"B.J. I'm still waiting." It was the gravelly voice of her agent. "Where's the manuscript you promised?"

"Ben." She placed the receiver in her other hand and wiped a sweaty palm on her shirt. "It isn't ready yet."

"You sound funny. What's wrong?"

"Nothing, Ben." She swallowed and wished her heart would stop hammering so wildly. She would have to tell him the truth soon. And face his wrath. "I'm busy. Can I call you back?"

"Why don't I come over?"

"No. I'm—going out."

"Where?"

"To my old house in New Jersey. My aunt lives there now. I promised her a visit."

"Can I see you tomorrow?"

She paused. "I'll call you, Ben."

She hung up the phone. With an angry gesture she rinsed the cup and went to search for her coat. She needed to get away from these four walls. They were closing in on her. She hadn't really planned to visit her aunt, but now that she had mentioned it, she felt the urge to see her old house. Besides, if she stayed here, she'd jump every time the phone rang. And the only person she wanted to hear from was never going to call.

As B.J. drove through the old neighborhood, her gaze swept the rows of houses. She had been right. They all looked the same. Same two stories, and postage-stamp-sized lawns. Same peeling paint. When she slowed and parked the car at the curb, she studied the little house where she had lived alone with her mother. There were special little touches she had forgotten that made this house unique. The large clay pot, now snow-covered, that her mother always planted with geraniums and ivy each spring. The big wooden C that her father had carved so many years ago. He had allowed B.J. to help him stain it before hanging it over the door.

Slowly she climbed from the car and made her way to the front door.

"Jessica." Her small, slim aunt, a replica of B.J.'s mother, beamed at the sight of her.

"I was in the neighborhood, and thought..." B.J. suddenly laughed in embarrassment and started over. "No, Aunt Jo, that isn't true. The fact is, I needed to see this house. I completed a book I've been working on. And suddenly it became important for me to come here. Can you understand that?"

Her aunt's arms opened wide. "Of course I can. Come in, child. I've missed you."

With a warm hug, her aunt led her through the small foyer to the living room. B.J. glanced around in appreciation. There were remnants of her mother's old furniture mingled with some of her aunt's pieces. The feeling was comfortable, homey.

"You've kept it cozy, Aunt Jo."

"I was so thrilled to have this house when you decided to move to New York." Her aunt gazed at the pictures on the mantel. "Your mother always loved this place so. It was the last home she shared with your father."

"Yes." B.J.'s voice sounded distant. Mentally shaking herself, she brightened. "Do you mind if I wander around?"

"Not at all. I'll make some tea."

B.J. glanced in the kitchen, then moved to the back porch, filled with wicker furniture and hanging plants. Even in the thin winter sunlight, the plants thrived in their warm, glass-enclosed room.

Wandering upstairs, B.J. looked into the master bedroom, where her aunt now slept. Across the hall she stepped into the room that had once been her bedroom. It was now a sewing room. Dropping onto the edge of the sofa bed, she studied the room where she had spent so many lonely nights. With a rush of feeling, it all came back to her.

Her father, splendid in his military uniform, opened the bedroom door. Light from the hall spilled over him, making him seem even larger than life.

"I'm leaving now, honey."

"Why?"

"I have to."

"No. No, you don't, Daddy."

"Hush now, honey. Don't make it harder on your mama." He chucked her under the chin. His little tomboy. "You've got to keep her smiling till I get back."

"She doesn't smile for me, Daddy. Only for you."

His voice lowered conspiratorially. "Then you've got to try harder, B.J. You're like me, you know. We can always put a good face on anything. You keep her smiling. Then, when I get back, we'll all have a good time together."

The thought struck with the clean thrust of a knife through her heart. "If you don't come back, all the laughter will die."

He tugged a lock of auburn hair, so like his own. "The laughter will never die, honey. It's here." He touched his heart, then hers. "Now, you take good care of your mama till I get back."

Don't go. The words were a shrill cry in her brain. Don't go. But she had held them back. She would be brave for him. Through a mist of tears, her chin trembling, she had given him a smile and a bleak, "'Bye, Daddy."

Agitated, B.J. strode to the window, seeing again her father's tall figure striding toward the car waiting at the curb to take him away on his mission.

As it sped away, the words thrust forth in a defiant shriek. "Don't go! I love you."

Maybe if she had shouted loudly enough all those years ago, she could have stopped him. He wouldn't have gone back to that war. He wouldn't have been lost to them forever. And her mother's laughter wouldn't have died.

Overcome with emotions she had repressed through the years, B.J. buried her face in her hands and wept.

Through a blur she watched the shiny Porsche pull up to the curb. The tall figure striding toward the house caused her heart to lurch. Numbly she turned from the window and heard the sound of his deep voice. For what seemed an eternity she stared at the wall, then turning, she hurried down the stairs.

Adam was standing in the small foyer, talking to her aunt. He studied B.J. as she stopped on the bottom step.

She looked even more beautiful than he remembered. Her hair was a cascade of russet curls that begged to be touched. Her green eyes gleamed almost too brightly, as if they had recently been washed with tears. Her mouth looked soft and vulnerable. He wanted to kiss it. It took all his willpower to keep from touching her. His hands clenched at his sides.

To hide her confusion, B.J. resorted to anger. "What brings you to this part of town, Adam? Slumming?"

"Always so quick with words, aren't you, Jess?" Ignoring her, Adam turned his charms on her aunt. "Has she always turned everything into a joke?"

"Just like her father." Aunt Jo gave Adam a radiant smile. "Come on inside, young man. I'm making some tea."

Turning to B.J., she muttered, "You should have told me you had such a good-looking man coming to visit.'' Touching her hair self-consciously, she said, ''I'll just be a few minutes.''

Alone with Adam, B.J.'s voice turned husky with anger. ''How did you find me?''

''I phoned your agent and threatened him with a lawsuit unless he agreed to give me this address.''

''Why?''

''I was afraid I wouldn't get to say all that needs saying before I leave.''

Her anger was replaced by a new surge of feelings. Adam was leaving. They had this one last chance to say goodbye.

Her tone softened. ''I'm sorry, Adam. After all you've been through, you don't need me to make it worse.'' She glanced at the floor. ''How are Flynn and Gerta doing?''

''Gerta is going to Gstaad to live with her niece. She said she'd still like to cook for me whenever I get to the chalet.''

He walked past her to the mantel and picked up a picture of B.J. and her parents, taken when she was nine. ''Flynn is going to travel for a year or two and relax at our cottage in France. I gave it to her. It was always her favorite. Then she's thinking of opening a small agency to train and place personal secretaries. She said it's a limited, but highly specialized and lucrative market.''

''I think that's a fine idea. Flynn has too much energy to retire.'' B.J. licked her lips. ''And you,

Adam? Are you"—she took a deep breath—"all healed and ready to resume your work?"

He set down the photo and met her look. "I've been busy tying up the loose ends before I leave."

Her heart sank at his words. Was that what she was? A loose end?

"I read the manuscript last night."

Her eyes widened.

"I didn't want to. I was afraid of what I'd find there. But I had to know it all."

Her mouth went dry. She had told him it was his, to do with as he pleased. And she meant it. Had it hurt him? Angered him? Had he tossed it in the fireplace when he finished it?

Adam turned, staring at the snow that gusted against the windowpane. He'd never be able to see snow again without thinking of Jess. "My mother was no fool. Her choice of biographer was brilliant."

He turned to see her mouth drop open in surprise.

"Anyone could relate the facts of her life. The press has been doing just that for days."

"She knew they would sensationalize her life and twist the facts."

He nodded. "While I was reading, I began to recall her first conversation with you in the library. She said she had actually begun to believe some of the things she had read about Vernon Allmon. And suddenly it dawned on me." Adam's words were harsh. "When she told me about my father, that night at the chalet, I felt shocked that she could betray her best friends. And somehow, I felt betrayed as well. But you managed to get inside her. For the first time, I understood why she did what she did."

"How do you feel now, knowing Josh Thompson was your father?"

Adam smiled. "Now that the initial shock is over, I can look at it all with more compassion. I was surprised. But I shouldn't be. He was always a father image. Always there when I needed him. And Carolyn was special in my life as well. She was like a second mother."

Adam's voice warmed with the memory of the manuscript he had stayed up all night to finish. "Carolyn and Josh were more than Mother's best friends. They became the extension of the family she craved. When she and Josh were thrown together during such a difficult time in both their lives, it was inevitable that they would turn to each other for comfort. What they couldn't foresee was the depth of passion that would surface just when they were at their most vulnerable. It must have nearly destroyed them both."

B.J. nodded, relieved that Adam understood, without judgment, without bitterness. "Josh was so in love with his wife, he couldn't accept her illness. He raged bitterly against it, doing everything in his power to find a cure. Nora was getting more and more caught up in the superstar syndrome and fearful that her chance for a normal marriage and motherhood was passing her by. She adored Josh and Carolyn, and wanted what they had. But when her chance for love came, she couldn't bear to think that she could be the instrument of their destruction.''

Adam moved to a small table littered with framed pictures of B.J. and her family. In each, the big man in the military uniform dominated the scene. He looked up to see B.J. watching him.

"According to your book, Josh and my mother were together for nearly forty years, and yet they never permitted themselves to express their passion except for that one desperate weekend. Do you think the reader will believe that?''

B.J. sighed. "I know it sounds almost heroic. But I believe it. Nora loved both Josh and Carolyn too much to ever allow her own needs to come between them. And she asked Josh to vow that he would take their secret to the grave rather than hurt his wife.''

"You make them sound like noble sinners.''

She shook her head. "Just human beings, Adam. To the world, they were superstars. To each other, they were just two people who found themselves in a painful situation. I think they made the best of it.''

He nodded. "So do I. And I wouldn't have believed anyone could write about such a tragic love affair and make it sound courageous. Even the circumstances of my birth, for the first time, sounded selfless instead of sordid.''

"There was nothing sordid about it." B.J. watched as he lifted still another picture to the light, avoiding her eyes. "Your mother was able to turn her back on her career because she wanted something else even more. Motherhood. Her movie-star image had become tarnished in her eyes. Hollywood had lost its appeal forever. And you became a focus of love for Carolyn and Josh, who couldn't have children together because of her illness. You even seemed to give purpose to Gerta and Klaus, as well as Flynn. Your birth may have been a scandal in Hollywood, but it was a blessing to a great many people."

"And your birth, Jess?"

She blinked. "I don't know what you mean."

"Before you came downstairs, your aunt was telling me that your father referred to you as B.J., Junior. You were his little tomboy, his special partner."

B.J. went very still. She had forgotten that. Was that why, all those years later, she had called herself B.J. instead of Jessica? She smiled at this sudden burst of knowledge. With it came new insight into herself.

Adam moved closer. "You expect me to calmly accept the fact that a man I knew all my life as a friend was actually my father. Yet you can't seem to forgive the father who was your best friend, because he had the nerve to follow his convictions."

"That's not true."

"Isn't it? Then who are you blaming all these years, Jess? Yourself?"

She turned away, stung by his words. He was too close to the truth. Hadn't she always wondered if she could have convinced her father to stay? Hadn't she always regretted all the words she hadn't spoken before he left? Had she ever told her father she loved him?

Aunt Jo paused in the doorway and discreetly coughed, to warn them of her presence. If she overheard, she gave no indication.

"Tea's ready." The older woman had removed her crisp apron to reveal a simple dress splashed with colorful flowers. "Warmed some biscuits, too," she said proudly. "I put up the jelly myself last summer."

Adam smiled and sat on the sofa, stretching his long legs out in front of him.

Aunt Jo beamed, enjoying the masculine company. She sat down beside him, pouring the tea.

"Come on, Jessica. These are your favorites."

B.J. smiled weakly at her aunt's obvious pleasure and took the chair across from them.

"Are you a writer, too, Adam?" Aunt Jo asked amiably.

"No. A photojournalist."

"Fancy word." She handed him a cup. "Does it pay well?"

He grinned. "Well enough."

"You thinking of courting Jessica?"

Adam's grin grew wider as B.J. gasped. He laughed, and took a sip of tea. There it was again. Courting. A nice, old-fashioned word, which held such appeal to him.

"I was."

"Was?" Both B.J. and her aunt spoke at the same time.

Adam spoke to Aunt Jo, as if B.J. weren't even there.

"Yes. I was thinking about it. But now that I've read her latest manuscript, I realize that she has a brilliant future. And I don't want to stand in the way of her career."

"Hmm." Aunt Jo considered his words for a moment, while she tasted her tea. When she looked up at him, her clear eyes sparkled. "Can't a woman write and be with a man too?"

"I suppose so," he mused. "But I have a job she hates. I think we'd probably spend a lot of time fighting about it."

"She hates your picture taking?"

Adam laughed. "No. She hates that I take my pictures in war zones."

The laughter left Aunt Jo's eyes. "You photograph wars?"

Adam nodded.

Her aunt glanced at B.J. and caught the look of pain on her niece's face.

"I see." She cleared her throat. Her tone grew gentle. With a glance in B.J.'s direction, she said, "It takes a special kind of love to endure that kind of profession. I once asked my sister how she could stand to live with a man who kept going off to war. Do you know what she said?"

Adam shook his head. B.J.'s hand froze on the handle of the cup. She stared at the floor.

"She said, 'Jo, after I fell in love with that man, there was no turning back. He's more than my lover; he's my best friend. I knew every time he left he might never return to me. I knew that I might spend a good many years alone. But real love means sharing, not controlling. I'd rather live alone the rest of my life, knowing I loved that man, than live a hundred years with anyone else.'"

Shocked, B.J.'s eyes met Adam's. His mother had said nearly the same thing on tape when she spoke of Adam's father.

"You couldn't consider some other line of work, I suppose?" the old woman asked to break the silence.

Adam set down his cup. "I've been offered a job as editor of the Washington bureau of *World News Magazine*. But I'm not sure if I should take it."

B.J. sat up straighter.

"Why?" her aunt asked.

Why? B.J.'s heart asked.

"I don't know." He shrugged. "I'm very good at what I do. I'm not so sure I'd like a desk job. I've always been in the thick of the action. Besides, I don't know anyone in Washington."

"That's the silliest reason I ever heard of." Aunt Jo touched a napkin to her lips. "How old are you, Adam?"

"Thirty-seven."

She stared into his expressionless eyes. "Old enough to know what you want and go after it." She stood. "I hear the kettle whistling."

"Aunt Jo," Adam called.

She turned.

"Thanks for the tea. I have to leave."

She smiled and walked away, leaving Adam and B.J. alone.

B.J. stood and walked Adam to the front door.

"I want you to publish the biography, Jess."

She nodded, feeling the lump in her throat beginning to grow. "When will you know about your job?"

He caught a strand of her hair and absently wrapped it around his finger. "What job?"

"The desk job."

"Oh." He stared down into her eyes. "I haven't given them an answer. I'm not sure I want to stay in one place for long."

"You could always go to Gstaad when you get eager to travel."

"I could. But even there I suppose I'd be lonely."

Her green eyes blazed with fire. "You mean you never get lonely in the jungle?"

"Sure I do. But there's nothing I can do about it there. I just have to tough it out until I get assigned to the next place."

She was growing angrier. "Maybe that's your trouble, Adam. You've never had to stick it out anywhere. When you get tired of one place, there's always someplace new and exciting to see."

His voice lowered. "There's never been a reason for me to stay in one place, Jess." The look he gave her sent tiny shivers of fire and ice along her spine. "Is there a reason for me to stay now?"

B.J. turned away sick at heart. "Goodbye, Adam. I wouldn't want to hold you back from your brilliant future."

"Goodbye, Jess." He bent nearer, until his lips were almost brushing her hair. He inhaled the familiar lemon fragrance. His warm breath feathered lightly across her cheek. "I have no doubt you'll be rich and famous some day."

She flinched and moved away. "You'll be very successful too, Adam. Maybe you can win another Pulitzer."

His lips thinned. He turned away and strode toward his car.

Aunt Jo stood in the hallway, her hands on her hips. "Is that all you can say to the man you love?"

B.J. whirled. "Love! Who says I love him?"

"Your eyes do. And that man wanted you to ask him to stay."

"I couldn't do that to Adam. I have no right to ask anything of him."

"Oh no?" Her aunt shook her head ruefully. "All those things you leave unsaid will stick in your throat forever, Jessica. Are you sure there's nothing you want to ask him?"

Suddenly, the scene she had recalled in her upstairs bedroom flashed through B.J.'s mind. Her father, standing so straight and tall in his military uniform. Her father, walking out the door. It was the last time she'd seen him. Adam, leaving for good. How could she live with that? How could she go on without him?

It was so simple, after all. B.J. pulled open the front door. Adam was stepping into his shiny Porsche.

"Adam."

He paused.

"Adam. Wait." She dashed across the snow-covered lawn and stopped at the curb. The cold air hurt her lungs. "Don't go."

He stared at her, long and hard, as if he didn't believe what he'd heard.

"Don't go, Adam, without giving me a chance to tell you that I love you." The words so long held back now tumbled from her lips. "I love you so much. I don't care where you go to do your work, as long as each time you return, you come back to me. That's all I want, Adam."

Incredulous, he walked closer, and took her in his arms. She was trembling. Her hair was a cloud of flame against the freshly falling snow. Her eyes were wide and misty with unshed tears.

"That's all I want too, Jess. To know that you love me. I could never walk away from you. I was trying right now. But the truth is, I had every intention of coming back and begging you to let us try again."

"I think I'm strong enough to let you go, Adam, as long as I know you love me."

She looked up to see the warmth of love in his eyes. He brushed her lips with his, and felt the need, hot, intense.

"But I don't think I'm strong enough to leave you, Jess, even for a little while." Against her temple he murmured, "How would you like to make your home in Washington?"

Laughing, she threw her arms around his neck. "Are you sure?"

He gathered her close, crushing her against the warmth of his body. "I'm not sure of anything except the fact that I love you. As long as you love me, too, we're going to make it."

He covered her mouth with his, and took the kiss deeper. Lifting his head, he murmured, "Get in the car. Quickly."

As he hustled her inside, she asked, "Why?"

"Because," he said, closing the door and climbing in the other side, "we've collected an audience."

She glanced up.

"Wave at your aunt."

Standing in the window, smiling broadly, stood Aunt Jo. On her face was a look of pure joy.

As B.J. waved he started the engine.

Two neighbor boys paused to point at the exotic car.

"The rest of what I have planned calls for privacy." He drew her close to him and nibbled an earlobe. "You can call your aunt from New York. Or should we go to Gstaad to be married?"

B.J. snuggled against him. Big wet snowflakes covered the windshield. She shivered with anticipation. It was going to be a glorious blizzard.

"Any place on earth, Adam. As long as I'm with you."

READERS' COMMENTS ON SILHOUETTE SPECIAL EDITIONS:

"I just finished reading the first six Silhouette Special Edition Books and I had to take the opportunity to write you and tell you how much I enjoyed them. I enjoyed all the authors in this series. Best wishes on your Silhouette Special Editions line and many thanks."

—B.H.*, Jackson, OH

"The Special Editions are really special and I enjoyed them very much! I am looking forward to next month's books."

—R.M.W.*, Melbourne, FL

"I've just finished reading four of your first six Special Editions and I enjoyed them very much. I like the more sensual detail and longer stories. I will look forward each month to your new Special Editions."

—L.S.*, Visalia, CA

"Silhouette Special Editions are — 1.) Superb! 2.) Great! 3.) Delicious! 4.) Fantastic! . . . Did I leave anything out? These are books that an adult woman can read . . . I love them!"

—H.C.*, Monterey Park, CA

*names available on request

If you're ready for a more sensual, more provocative reading experience…

We'll send you **4** Silhouette Desire novels

FREE…

and without obligation

Then, we'll send you six more Silhouette Desire® novels to preview every month for 15 days with absolutely no obligation!

When you decide to keep them, you pay just $1.95 each ($2.25, in Canada), *with no shipping, handling, or additional charges of any kind!*

Silhouette Desire novels are not for everyone. They are written especially for the woman who wants a more satisfying, more deeply involving reading experience.

Silhouette Desire novels take you *beyond* the others and offer real-life drama and romance of successful women in charge of their lives. You'll share precious, private moments and secret dreams... experience every whispered word of love, every ardent touch, every passionate heartbeat.

As a home subscriber, you will also receive FREE, a subscription to the Silhouette Books Newsletter as long as you remain a member. Each issue is filled with news on upcoming titles, interviews with your favorite authors, even their favorite recipes.

And, the first 4 Silhouette Books are absolutely FREE and without obligation, yours to keep! What could be easier... and where else could you find such a satisfying reading experience?

To get your free books, fill out and return the coupon today!

Silhouette ♥ Desire®

Silhouette Special Edition

COMING NEXT MONTH

SUMMER DESSERTS—Nora Roberts
Blake Cocharan wanted the best, and Summer Lyndon was a dessert chef *extraordinaire*. She had all of the ingredients he was looking for, and a few he didn't expect.

HIGH RISK—Caitlin Cross
Paige Bannister had lived life from a safe distance until she met rodeo rider Casey Cavanaugh and found herself taking risks she had never thought she would dare.

THIS BUSINESS OF LOVE—Alida Walsh
Working alongside executive producer Steve Bronsky was a challenge that Cathy Arenson was willing to meet, but resisting his magnetic charm was more than a challenge—it was an impossibility.

A CLASS ACT—Kathleen Eagle
Rafe had always thought that Carly outclassed him, but when she was caught in a blizzard nothing mattered other than warming her by his fire...and in his arms.

A TIME AND A SEASON—Curtiss Ann Matlock
Two lovers were thrown together on a remote Oklahoma highway. Katie found Reno easy to love, but could she embrace life on his ranch as easily as she embraced him?

KISSES DON'T COUNT—Linda Shaw
Reuben North hadn't planned on becoming involved, but when Candice's old boyfriend threatened to take her child away, Reuben found himself comfortably donning his shining armor.

AVAILABLE NOW:

THE HEART'S YEARNING
Ginna Gray

STAR-CROSSED
Ruth Langan

A PERFECT VISION
Monica Barrie

MEMORIES OF THE HEART
Jean Kent

AUTUMN RECKONING
Maggi Charles

ODDS AGAINST TOMORROW
Patti Beckman